E. P. Henrichs's

THE ADVENTURES OF DETECTIVE PACKARD AND THE ROCKS

~ 2 ~

The Adventures of Detective Packard and the Rocks

ISBN - 979-8-9916620-0-0

Illustrated by E. P. Henrichs and J. T. Henrichs

Edited by B. J. Henrichs

Character Ideas by Z. E. Henrichs

Cover Design and Art. E.P. Henrichs

Table of Contents

Characters

Joey Packard – Main character, NOPD Detective

Roc – Joey's partner and buddy, brother to Ks

Ks (pronounced K·S) – Joey's partner and more hyperactive buddy, brother to Roc

Radford Weston – Joey's good friend and detective partner, Senior NOPD Detective

Scooter Ford – Friend to Joey and Radford, a young skilled auto technician

Klaus Abel – Head of the Abel's household, father to Alice and Bert

Alice – Sister to Bert, the older child of the Abel twins

Bert – Brother to Alice, younger of the Abel twins

Maria Abel – Mother to Bert and Alice, wife to Klaus

Mr. Gregory Woods– Brother to Ivan Woods, brother-in-law to Irene Woods

Irene Woods – Wife to Ivan Woods, mother to Ruth, Smith, Amy and Haley

Chief Albert A. Anderson – New Orleans Chief of Police

Officer Eric Garrison – Grizzled, but friendly gentleman, NOPD officer

Officer Claire Cromwell – Garrison's partner, NOPD officer

Officer Nathan Richards – Loyal NOPD officer

Tommy Lee – Best friend to Ricky, co-host of the YouTube channel, "The Dudes' Discoveries"

Ricky – Best friend to Tommy Lee, host of the YouTube channel, "The Dudes' Discoveries"

Ardanan – Gang leader, leader to many gangs, right hand to Mr. Gregory

Parker – Driver

Herbert and Norman – Men who work for Ardanan

Clarkson – Mr. Gregory's most trusted man, second to Ardanan

Bill – The muscle of the gang

Stan – The brains of the gang

Frank – The gunman of the gang

Ivan Woods- Husband to Irene Woods, Father to Ruth, Smith, Amy, and Haley

Dedication and thanks to my family,

And to Jesus, my Creator.

The Adventures of Detective Packard and the Rocks

Chapter 1: The Ruby Cat

Birds sang in the bright, blue sky. Clouds happily floated overhead. A warm breeze whistled through the air. It was another beautiful day in Lafayette Square, New Orleans. Hundreds of people had flocked to the park for the dedication of the New Orleans Museum, which was nearing completion. The convention, hosted by the city's own mayor, Arnold Green, had drawn a large crowd from all over the city. After the ceremonies and speeches concluded, some of the vendors had set up tents for everyone to look at their art and antiques. As in many town park events, there was a lot of selling, bartering, and auctioneering going on. Food tents were also set up, serving delicious food to the hungry shoppers. There was an array of foods to choose from, deep fried chicken, fresh local seafood, and exotic foods from around the world.

A young detective, the age of twenty-four, walked down the main sidewalk through the park. Spiked, brown hair covered the top of his head, and bushy eyebrows gave expression to his appearance. For a young man, he had a maturity that the town folk respected. In addition to his mature look, he had a corresponding attitude, which the citizens respected. He wore a dark, nougat leather trench coat, covering his signature, long-sleeved, orange-brown shirt.

Following behind him were two animated rocks, each having round eyes, stubby arms and legs, and big grins. No one from the city seemed scared or worried about these incredible partners. The citizens knew them well for being such a great Detective of the New Orleans Police Department in the past several years. The detective and his rock partners were proud of their city. It was an amazing place, never boring, never quiet, something was always happening.

He and his partners walked between the vendors' tents, looking at the different setups. A glimmer of sunlight shone off a statue and caught the detective's eye. He walked over to the setup hosted by an elderly couple. Their tables had all kinds of antiques, from the 18th century to 20th century items.

He read the description of the cat statue: "*There could be rubies in this statue that could yield the buyer a fortune! Legend says that a crook hid rubies in a statue just like this one.*" The detective looked up at the elderly gentleman who ran the booth. The gentleman was grizzled thin man with a wide brim hat perched atop his head, his cheeks were sunken into his face.

"Hey, sir, is this true?" the detective asked.

The old man looked at him through his small rectangular glasses, "Aye, Joey Packard," he said through a thick southern accent, "That's what the legen' says."

"So, it is true," replied Joey.

The elderly woman spoke up from behind the table, "Go on, Charles; tell 'em the story."

"A'ight, Janis," he chuckled, adjusting his wide brimmed hat, "Now there's a true story from 1894 about a famous jewel pickin' thief from Germany by the name of Klaus Gudden. He had two twin matchin' rubies that firstly came from an old statue in a Korean temple built around 165 A.D. In 1560, the ol' sultan of the Ottoman Empire acquired 'em, who in turn gave them to a lady of his court after she had…er…let me just say, she pleased him in some ways 'un night. But the rubies cost the lady her life, ya know. A no feel'n jewel thief killed her to get his hands on them. The rubies were lost in time after that. Somehow, about 200 years later, we find that they belonged to Louis XV, who gave 'em to Madame Pompadour. She later sold them to a Russian nobleman."

"So, how did Klaus Gudden obtain the rubies?" asked Joey, "The rubies seem to be just appearing and reappearing in different hands throughout history."

"That's the thing," replied the gentleman. "Nobody known a thing how he got them. He appeared in Berlin one day, and the police caught 'im. He tried to escape but was pitifully shot in the process. And know what they foun'?"

"The rubies, I bet," answered Roc, the larger of the two rocks.

"Nothin'!" said the old man. "The rubies weren't on him! So, a few years later, a gem exper' named Michael Graves had been try'n to find the rubies. He reasoned that rubies of that value couldn' just disappear. So, he began to look for 'em. Mr. Graves learned that while the police set their dragnet, Gudden was trapped in a certain block in ol' Berlin. He had been there for seven days. Graves sniffed for clues in that area and found out Gudden had swung by a little ceramic factory, which specialized in makin' ceramic cats. Graves also learned that Gudden had specially prepared a cat statue to be glazed and had examined the thang carefully. The owner remembered that this certain cat was still wet and soft, since it had just been taken out of the mold. He made that owner promise that the cat be sold to nobody else, you see. The perp also etched a small X underneath the statue's base so he would remember it, and sayin' that he would be back for it in the week. The ceramic maker told Graves that when the strange customer didn' come back, he shipped that cat with a hundred of the others to America. Graves assumed that Gudden must have pushed the rubies into the soft clay of the cat. Knowin' this, Graves desperately began his search for the cat."

He sat down, "That's where this here story ends. The owner of that shop shipped thousands of the statues to here in America. This cat I have here might be one of them. And all of this happened o'er a hundred years ago, leaving the trail to find the Ruby Cat cold. Only the devil himself knows where it might be. Heck, some could've been shipped back to ol' Europe. The cats are eight inches high, with their tails wrapped around their forepaws. That's just one description though. Some descriptions say the cat itself is in a sleepin' position. It's full of contradictions and unsolved mysteries."

He pointed to his statue, "As you can see, this particular 'un used to be a yellowish color, but now it's old and scratched up. The "X" ain't no longer visible."

"Wow, so this may be one!" exclaimed Ks, the smaller of the two rocks.

"Yep," said the old man.

"Come on, Ks," Joey said doubtfully, "this is obviously just a far-fetched folk legend if you ask me,"

"Ha, if it's proof you want to prove it's true, I have it right here," the man reassured him.

The man grabbed his laptop from the table and opened it. He tapped on a few keys and turned the laptop around to show Joey. Joey leaned in to get a good look.

"'Ight here," he said, "An old newspaper, *The Spokesman's Review*, 1959 publication. It says 'ere that the Ruby Cat's rubies had been estimated to be around five hundred thousand dollars…that's around five million or so in today's money."

Joey eyed the paper on the screen. Sure enough, on the internet's archive of old newspaper publications, there was an article written on the Ruby Cat. A photo of two men holding a plaster cat was shown in the article. Joey leaned back and thought for a moment; this gave the whole legend quite a bit more credibility.

"How much is it?" asked Joey.

"'Bout $100," replied the old man, "Since the rubies might be inside, and I'm pretty sure this might be the one."

Joey raised an eyebrow and searched his pockets, "I can give you $60," he said.

The elderly gentleman rubbed his chin, "Hmm…I don't know…Due to chance of the rubies inside it could be worth a whole lotta more…"

"Let him have it, Charles," interrupted the elderly woman, "The reason why we're sellin' it here is to get rid of the dad-gum thing."

"You've always been right, Janice!" chuckled the old man. He turned to Joey, "Deal! Yours for $60!"

Joey handed him the cash and the old man gave him the cat statue.

At that moment, a pale, even older gentleman with a cane hobbled through the crowd. He was thin as a skeleton with a long, frizzly beard. He wore an old tux and a small-brimmed hat with spectacles on his nose. He spotted the cat and hurried over to Joey.

"Ah!" he exclaimed, "Don't buy the statue! It needs to be destroyed! A curse is upon it!"

"A curse," questioned Joey, "What do you mean, sir?"

"Just as I said," he franticly repeated, "There is a curse on it!"

He staggered away into the crowd shouting, "A curse is on the cat statue! Don't buy it!" A group of people around him moved out of his path and watched as he made his way through.

Joey turned to Mr. Charles, "What does he mean by a curse?"

"Bah, that's just old Tom," replied the man, "He believes the old gag about the curse. I just think it's a tall tale."

"Oh, well then, thank you, sir," said Joey, as he and the rocks walked away.

"There goes another youngster, seeking treasure," said the man as he and wife watched the detective leave.

"Just like all the others, Charles," replied Janice.

Joey examined the statue on the walk towards home. The rocks gazed at it all the way.

"We'll be rich!" exclaimed Ks.

"Now, let's not jump to conclusions yet," said Joey, "We don't know if there's rubies or not in this statue. We could get rich, or we could be left with a broken statue. This all could just be lore and folktales."

"I guess so," Ks sighed, "but hopefully it's not just a legend!"

Joey looked up and spotted a man in a green coat watching him from across the street. He nodded to Joey and Joey nodded back. The man then ambled towards a parked car near the curb of the street. The driver in the car gave him a wink and the man climbed into the back seat. The driver cranked the engine, and they sped away.

Chapter 2: Mystery

Joey and the rocks arrived at their home; a twelve-story apartment complex on the street corner. He entered the building, waved to Miss Jane and Ms. Mary, the women at the front desk, and ascended the stairs to his apartment. He unlocked the door, crossed the apartment's small living room, and put the statue on a bookshelf.

Joey was also a guy who took an interest in historical artifacts, and the bookshelf contained many artifacts from around the world. The new cat statue perfectly fit in his collection. He removed his coat and hung it on the coat rack. The rocks climbed up to the top of the shelf and they and Joey took a good look at the statue.

"Just think," exclaimed Ks still enthusiastic about the rubies, "There could be millions of dollars' worth of rubies inside!"

"You're right," agreed Joey, "it would be nice to get a couple million dollars or so, not going to lie. Let me get my magnifying glass."

Joey walked to his desk drawer to grab his magnifying glass. He shuffled through the contents of the drawer until he found it. Now this wasn't your old Sherlock Holmes magnifying glass, this was a digital scanner, with fingerprint analysis technology. It was in the shape of a tablet, only a little wider. It could also magnify things even better than an ordinary magnifying glass could. He

switched it on and looked at the statue through the screen, moving up and down in slow motion. The scanner emitted a low, humming noise.

"See anything special?" asked Ks.

"Not really," replied Joey, "I was looking the X on the bottom, but I couldn't find it." Joey turned off the scanner and placed it on the table. "If it did have the X, it would be probably worn off by now due to age," he added.

Joey headed to the fridge and pulled out a box of birdseed. He walked over to a round-topped cage at a corner of his apartment's living room.

"Hello, Pauley," he said, "How are you doing today?"

"Pauley wants seeds! Pauley wants seeds!" the parrot within the cage squawked.

Joey poured the seeds into Pauley's wooden food dish, while Ks got Pauley some fresh water. Pauley tried to open the gate as Ks put the water into the cage. Ks held his hand up to stop the bird.

"No, Pauley," scolded Ks. He looked at Joey, "We've got to put a lock on this cage, or he'll get out."

"We will," Joey agreed, "We'll buy one today after we visit the library to gather more information about the Ruby Cat."

"Which one?" asked Roc.

"The New Orleans Public Library," Joey responded, "It has one of the largest book collections in the city."

Joey grabbed his coat and he and the rocks headed out the door. After they left their apartment, they hurried down the sidewalk towards the library.

Several minutes later, they were walking into the building. Joey knew he would be here awhile, but he didn't mind. He liked the smell of old books and looking through the yellowed pages. He always learned something new about mystery he was researching. He strolled down the aisles as he scanned for any book that might have information about the Ruby Cat. *Not here*, he would say to himself repeatedly as he looked. He heard a voice above him and looked up.

"Here's one," exclaimed Ks on the top shelf, "It's a treasure book! It should have plenty of information about the statue!"

Ks held the book in the air, pointed to the cover. However, the book was large and heavy, and he lost his balance. He started tumbling down, down, down, which in turn, made more books fall. Joey and Roc jumped out of the way of the cascading books as the they thumped to the ground.

A chorus of a loud "SHHH!" came from all the library patrons around them.

"Sorry," Joey apologized. He looked at Ks, buried under the books.

"Are you all right, 'tome dome'?" he asked.

"Yeah," moaned Ks, still dizzy.

After they returned the books to their proper places, Joey and the rocks went to a table to sit down and read the book Ks had found. The green lamp above shone brightly down upon them. Joey quickly flipped the pages, looking for information on the Ruby Cat.

"Here it is, Rocks!" he exclaimed, pausing at a picture of the Ruby Cat.

He started reading the text quietly to the rocks, so no one else would overhear.

"The story dates to 165 A.D., a time of unrest in Korea when the country was in the grip of bitter struggles between warring branches of the same ruling family. Towards the end of that year a band of brigands loosely attached to one of the armies raided a temple, killing the monks and making off with two perfect rubies, probably the eyes of some sacred statue. The gems then disappeared from history till 1560 when they were acquired by the Sultan of the Ottoman Empire who gave them to a lady of his court…"

Joey flipped through a few more pages of the book, "And the rest of the story is pretty much the same thing the old gentleman told us at the town park…. wait, right here, this is what that old man in the market square was hollering about!"

Joey read on enthusiastically, "'People are afraid to investigate this mystery further because of a superstition that the rubies were cursed by the Korean temple priests. They also don't want to be hunted down by treasure seekers.' Well, how about that?"

"So," said Roc, "Where does that leave us?"

"Not sure," replied Joey as he turned the pages, "But the first thing to do is examine the statue better for more clues; dust for fingerprints, scan some more, and test to determine if the statue is hollow."

The evening grew late into the night, and the library was now closing.

"Man, it's already eight o'clock," he said looking at his watch, "Come on rocks, we better go home."

During all this, a dark silhouette was watching them outside through the window. Joey put the book down to rest his eyes and peered out the window. As he looked, his eye caught the movement of a man in the shadows. Realizing he had been spotted, the man bolted away! Joey slipped his coat on.

"Hurry, rocks!" he shouted, "Someone is spying on us!"

"What?!" exclaimed the rocks but wasted no time following Joey out the library door.

The mystery man ran down the block and around a corner. He slowed down, thinking he had lost them. Just as he glanced over his shoulder, the detective and his partners burst around the corner.

"There he is!" shouted Ks, as they continued the chase.

The man picked up speed sprinting down an alley, jumping over boxes and old wooden crates with Joey close behind. He hurled a trashcan into Joey's path, but Joey sped up and leapt over it.

"It would do you good to stop!" shouted Joey.

The man exploded out of the end of the alley and into the street where an old car was waiting. He hopped in the car, slamming the door.

"Hurry, hurry!" he shouted to the driver, "They're after us!"

The driver nodded and floored into traffic and sped down the street.

"Confound it all!" Joey gasped, "He got away!'

"But we can still track them down," added Roc, "We know their car is a 1970 blue Cadillac Fleetwood."

"You're right," said Joey, "We'll follow them down this road."

Joey and the rocks trotted down the street that the car escaped on. Joey took out his scanning device, which he called the SD. He bent over the spot where the Cadillac squealed out and scanned the tire tracks. The blue light from the device shown on the ground like a flashlight. They walked for a while examining the tracks through the device. It was dark now, and the moon was big, blue, and bright. Eventually the tracks led them to a large driveway, blocked by a gate. Behind the gate sat an old mansion, surrounded by lush forests. An old cinderblock wall surrounded the mansion grounds. On the wall near the gate was a vine-covered sign that read *"Mansion of the Woods"*. A rusted iron buzzer was next to the sign. Joey pushed the button a few times and waited. Roc and Ks sat next to the wall and gazed up at the stars. Joey looked through the gate to see if anyone was coming, but no one arrived. Joey rang the bell a few more times, but to no avail.

"Huh, strange," said Joey, "Either the buzzer isn't working, or we are being ignored."

"Most likely the latter," sighed Roc, still star gazing.

"Well, let's try something else," Joey replied.

He took a step back and examined the wall's height. Joey tried jumping up the walls to grab a foothold, but just slipped off the side.

"Hey, give me a hand, will you?" said Joey, "This wall is too high for me to reach the edge."

"We can't give you a hand, but we'll give a head!" said Roc with his crooked grin.

Joey didn't laugh.

Joey stood on top of the rocks to make a second attempt to reach the wall's edge. He leapt up again, grabbed the edge, and scrambled to the top of the wall. He made sure the coast was clear on the other side and jumped down to the ground.

"Alright, boys," he whispered, "I'm in!"

Chapter 3: The Mansion

The enormous mansion, that looked like something out of the 19th century, was well worn with age. Vines crawled along the walls, and the paint was flaking. The mansion's tall, pointed roof had a huge chimney on one side. Above the front porch was a decrepit balcony, which didn't look like it could hold anyone at all anymore. Two columns stood guard beside the front doors.

Surrounding the mansion was a large yard, which in times past hosted beautiful gardens, but was now overgrown with tall weeds. A long driveway led down the middle of the expansive lawn to the front steps.

Joey walked up the steps to the big double doors and gave a knock on one of the doors. He looked around the property as he waited for someone to answer. His eyes fell on the tall trees that bordered the entire front lawn. *This is why it's probably called "Woods' Mansion",* he thought. The door opened, interrupting his thoughts. A man in a black uniform stood in the doorway. Joey assumed he was the butler of the house. The man looked surprised that Joey was inside the property.

"Hello, how did you get past the gate?" he asked in a gruff voice.

"Um, yeah," Joey replied, "I rang on the bell, but no one came..."

"I'm sorry for the inconvenience," the butler said, interrupting, "The gate buzzer must be broken."

"Very inconvenient," Joey said, nodding his head, still having his doubts about being ignored earlier.

"How can I help you?" the butler asked.

"I would like to talk to the owners," Joey said, "I need to ask them a few questions."

"Of course, sir," the butler said, slowly. He motioned his hand towards the mansion's lobby, "Please, come in."

Joey walked into the lobby and the butler shut the double doors with a loud clunk. The butler then led him into the massive living room.

"I'll be back with them in a few minutes," he said, and then left down the hall.

Joey looked around the living room. It sure was an impressive sight, despite being in disrepair. He decided to inspect the living room while he waited. He entered the massive living room and took in the view. An old grandfather clock, along with numerous paintings and photos, hung on the walls. Joey looked closer at one picture, which portrayed a young woman sitting on a chair. A man, which Joey assumed to be her husband, stood next to her with hands behinds his back. Two neatly dressed boys stood on either side of them. Each person had their names printed below them. The man, Jack Woods, the woman, Marian Woods. The boys, Ivan and Gregory. The next picture showed the family in a large group of people. They appeared to be at a Christmas banquet. The last, largest photo was uniquely different from the others, in the sense that it didn't show any celebrations. Instead, the photo presented two boys at a funeral. One boy was noticeably older than the other, by at least ten years. Both lads looked similar despite their age difference, so Joey assumed they were brothers. The boys were accompanied by a group of people gathered round a coffin. On top of the coffin a plaque read *"Jack Woods, 1952-1992."*

"So, this is why this mansion is named *"Woods' Mansion,"* he whispered to himself.

Joey was intrigued by all the photos he had seen. He next turned his attention to the formal dining room, which was adjacent to the living room. He walked out of the room and into the dining room. Next to a large window which overlooked the front lawn, there was an impressive, yet dusty, dining table surrounded by many chairs. Joey stood in the dining room's center and looked around. His eye caught something on the dining room table.

"Cat statues!" he exclaimed.

On the table sat a row of three identical cat statues. They were worn and faded due to the passing of time. Joey realized something was different though, these were in the sleeping position, very different from his statue which was in a sitting position. Joey picked up one and looked it over.

"Looks like a plaster cat statue, just like mine!" exclaimed Joey, "Is someone else trying to find the rubies?"

As he held the statue, he stepped on something that made a small, cracking noise. He looked down and saw, to his amazement, small pieces of what looked like a broken statue.

Joey tried to put the statue back together. A few pieces were missing, so Joey looked around for a trashcan. He saw one, an old, rusted pail, and peered inside. Sure enough, the missing pieces were inside. He put the whole statue together and it was indeed the same as his Ruby Cat.

"It's like that old gent said," Joey whispered to himself, "There's conflicting reports on whether the statue was in a sleeping position or sitting pose. For all I know, the statue I had was completely the wrong type. Or perhaps I am running around like a fool chasing a made-up legend…"

Just then, he heard voices and footsteps.

"Spigots," muttered Joey. "They're returning."

He gently put the statue pieces back into the trashcan and sprinted out the door back to the living room. He returned just in time as the butler and a man came down the stairs and into the room. The black-haired man wore a brown suit with a bright red bow tie. He also wore tennis shoes, which did not match his clothes in the slightest.

"Hello," he said, straightening his bow tie, "My name is Joesph Benard, what can I do for you?"

"Good day, sir," Joey replied, "My name is Joey Packard. Earlier I was at the library when I noticed someone spying on me through the windows. My comrades and I followed him, and he drove away in a blue

1970 Cadillac. However, they raced off so quickly that we couldn't catch them. I traced the tire marks with this device here, which led me to this mansion."

"Interesting," the man said, rubbing his chin, "We surely don't own a blue Cadillac."

"Oh?" Joey asked, "Well, do you mind if I look at the car? Maybe we got the color wrong."

"Certainly," Mr. Benard agreed, "I don't mind."

The three walked out the front double doors and headed to the big garage in back. The man looked at Joey with a side-eye.

"It's most peculiar why you came here," he stated, "What is the device that led you here?"

"This one right here," Joey answered, pulling the scanner out of his coat, "It's used by the New Orleans Police."

"Oh!" the man exclaimed, and slapped Joey on the back. "You're that detective who works for Chief Albert A. Anderson. I knew the name Joey Packard sounded familiar. Yes, that device of yours must be foolproof then."

"Uh, yes, it's very reliable," gasped Joey.

They reached garage and the butler pulled open one of the doors. He then flipped on the light switch and Joey and Mr. Benard walked in. To Joey's amazement, the only car within was just an old black Buick sedan.

"No, it isn't the car we saw," Joey pondered.

"Interesting," the man said, patting his hand on the Buick, "I guess your scanner was faulty, which is surprising for a device of law enforcement.

"It sure is, sir," Joey agreed, "By the way, excuse me for being curious, but I saw some cat statues on your dining room table. Do you collect statues? There were a few pieces on the floor as well."

"I just like collecting cat statues from all over the world," Mr. Benard replied with a shrug, "There are plenty of them with all different shapes and sizes. It's an obsession of mine I can't break, sadly. And the one on the floor broke when, ironically, my cat knocked it over."

"Oh, I see," said Joey, "Well, it's getting late, and I have to go. Thank you for your time, gentlemen. Sorry to bother you."

"My pleasure," Mr. Benard said, "The good butler will open the gates for you. Hope you find the man you were looking for."

"Thanks," said Joey, turning to leave.

The butler had already arrived at the gates and opened them. Joey waved goodbye as he left. The butler went back inside the mansion and closed the doors. Roc and Ks stopped stargazing and focused their attention on Joey.

"So," Ks asked, "Were they the ones?"

"No," replied Joey, "This isn't the right house."

"Not the right house? What about the scanner," Roc added, puzzled, "it led us this way?"

"It must have made some sort of mistake," answered Joey, tapping the scanner with his knuckles. "The car in the garage was a completely different make and model. Unless the Cadillac was hidden somewhere, and they're lying about it. Anyway, it's time to hit the road home."

The rocks agreed and they all headed down the sidewalk back to the apartment.

The night was quiet, the moon bright, and the trees around the mansion whistled in the wind. Hidden in the trees to the side of the mansion, a sudden gust of wind blew a tarp off a large object. That object underneath the tarp was the 1970 blue Cadillac.

Chapter 4: More Mystery

Joey and the rocks returned to their apartment an hour later. It was after midnight, and most of the tenants in the apartment complex were already asleep.

"It makes no sense," said Joey as he sluggishly climbed the stairs to their apartment on the fourth floor. "What caused the scanner to make such a blatant mistake?"

Joey pulled a key out of his pocket and unlocked the door to find Pauley, his parrot, free from the confines of his cage and flying around in the room!

"Oh, no!" cried Roc, "I knew we should have put that new lock on sooner!"

"We have to get him back in his cage!" exclaimed Ks.

"Right," said Joey as he reached for a towel, "I'll use this to grab him."

Joey leaned in with the towel just behind Pauley. Pauley turned his head, saw Joey coming, and flew away!

"Spigots," Joey muttered and tried again.

"We'll scare him your way," said the rocks.

Roc and Ks climbed on top of the shelf where Pauley was perched. Joey came around on the other side of the shelf. Roc and Ks leaped after Pauley, herding him towards Joey, who stood with the towel at the ready. Joey dove at Pauley. Pauley swooped to the left and Joey and the rocks collided heads! Joey dropped to the ground, rubbing his head. He saw literal stars.

Suddenly, he saw that Pauley was heading straight towards the Ruby Cat!

"No, Pauley!" shouted Joey, but it was too late.

Pauley fluttered into the Ruby Cat, causing it to fall off the shelf and hurtle to the ground. Crack! The Ruby Cat shattered into a million pieces.

"Pauley!' exclaimed Ks, "Look at what you did!"

"It's not a Ruby Cat anymore," said Joey as he picked up the pieces. Then he noticed something.

"Look, Rocks," he said, "This is not the cat with the rubies."

"That's right!" exclaimed Ks.

"Yes, this one is empty," added Joey, "Thanks to our feathered friend we found that out…"

He turned and frowned at Pauley. The green bird with yellow wings looked at Joey as if to say, "So what?" Joey glared back.

"Well, Rocks, we have a lot of work to do," he said, "Tracking down the real Ruby Cat is going to be a challenge."

He swept up the pieces and put the statue on a shelf to maybe, with any luck, glue it back together later. After the mess was cleaned up, Joey locked Pauley in the cage with the new lock they had bought. Exhausted from the day, he laid down on the couch and slowly drifted to sleep.

****

The sound of crackling and sizzling roused Joey from his sleep. He sniffed the air, filled with a delicious smell of eggs and bacon. Joey looked at the clock hanging on the wall by the window that showed it was 9:08 am. He got up from the couch and trudged to the small kitchen to find the rocks making breakfast.

"You were sleeping in later than usual and we knew you would be hungry, so we decided to make breakfast," said Roc.

"Why, thank you, Rocks," Joey said gratefully.

After breakfast, Joey turned on the TV to the news channel. It had nothing new, except the same old news on politics, crimes, and weather. Joey shut off the TV. At that moment, the doorbell to his apartment rang. Joey opened the door to find Officers Claire Cromwell and Eric Garrison of the New Orleans Police Department at his door.

"Hello, Joey," they both said. They sounded rather irritated.

"Hi, Claire, Eric," replied Joey in a cheerful tone, trying to lighten the mood, "Come in and have a seat."

He offered to hang their hats on the rack as the officers walked into his apartment. The rocks handed them glasses of iced tea, and they sat down on Joey's big brown sofa. Joey pulled up a stool and sat down across from them to start the discussion.

"So, what is the news today?" he asked.

"Kind of the same, we've been responding to the recent sporadic break-ins in the area," replied Officer Cromwell.

"More carjackings?" asked Joey.

"No," replied Officer Garrison, "House break-ins, but the funny thing is, the thieves didn't take anything."

"Huh," Joey raised an eyebrow, "That's odd."

"I know," responded Officer Cromwell, "Even weirder is the link between all the break-ins."

"What's the link?" asked Joey.

"The owners of the houses are all antique collectors, or related to collecting in some way, of antique items," Clarie answered.

"So, they aren't just stealing whatever they can get their hands on," Joey pondered, "They are looking for a particular item?"

"You got that right," replied Officer Garrison, "The top brass, Chief Anderson himself, has ordered all officers to be on a lookout for these crooks."

"We don't have any leads about their identities or their whereabouts," said Officer Cromwell. She sipped her tea, "And what is the item they are looking for, we have no idea."

"No possible answers cross my mind either," Joey added, rubbing his chin. He then froze, "Except one thing, but it's a long shot."

Just then, Eric's walkie-talkie burst out noisily.

"Break-in at house, 415 25th street!" the dispatcher exclaimed over the speaker, "Unit 504, respond immediately, over!"

"That's us!" said Officer Garrison and gulped down the last of his tea.

"Yes," replied Claire, she set her cup down on the table, "Goodbye, Joey! We'll talk to you later."

The two jumped up from the couch, grabbed their hats off the rack, and raced out the door.

"Alrighty, see you later, officers," Joey called.

"See you around!" exclaimed the rocks as the two officers headed down the stairs of the apartment building. They burst out of the lobby to their patrol cars and sped away on their call.

"Rocks," said Joey as he closed the door, "this mystery just keeps getting deeper and more dangerous. We had better find that Ruby Cat quickly. The sooner we get our hands on the statue, the sooner those thieves realize the jig is up. No Ruby Cat, no reason to ransack people's houses."

"Rats," said Roc with a sigh, "Now we'll never get a break!"

Chapter 5: Off to Berlin

Joey sat down at the computer to organize all the facts he had gathered in order of oldest to newest. He leaned back and started to put the puzzle together in his mind.

"Hmm," he said to himself. "An ancient statue with rubies for eyes, that came from the Ottoman Empire. The rubies were taken from the statue and passed down to other people of royalty over the centuries. A notorious, jewel thief stole the rubies, only to be cornered and killed in a shoot-out with the police in a small shop in Berlin. However, before his demise, he hid them inside a ceramic cat statue. The statue was shipped to America with many other statues like it. The rubies could still be in the statue anywhere in the world. Nevertheless, people are afraid to investigate this mystery because of the fear of being stalked by curses or unsavory characters. Now, house burglaries are occurring, but the thieves aren't taking any belongings. Instead, they seem to be looking for something, but no one knows what."

"Well, we got a lot on our plate!" exclaimed Ks.

Joey nodded and got up from the computer. He paced back and forth a few times while thinking to himself.

"First plan of action," Joey said, raising his finger, "we need to visit Berlin."

"Berlin! You mean, as in Berlin, Germany?" shuddered Roc, "That's a long way off!"

"Yes," replied Joey, "but that's where this whole story originated from, so it would be a logical step to start there."

The rocks muttered their reluctant agreement.

"So," said Joey, "We should leave very soon, as a matter of fact, first thing tomorrow morning. Now, let's get our baggage together."

Joey went to his closet, shuffling through it to pull out his suitcase. He began packing clothes and other things necessary for travel. One thing he knew for sure, this would be a lot of work for him and the rocks on their own. Suddenly, an idea hit him! He could take the town's famous detective, Radford, with him to Germany. Joey pulled out his phone and dialed the well-known detective.

"Hello?" came the voice of an older man with a heavy Boston accent.

"Hello, Mr. Radford! This is Joey, how are you?"

"Hello there, Joey! I'm just fine. Now what are you and the rocks up to during your vacation?"

"That's just why I was calling…"

Joey explained to Radford everything that had happened. He told him of how he had stumbled onto the mystery of the two matching rubies. He also informed Radford that other shady people were interested in the rubies as well.

"So, do you think you can help with my quest?" he asked, "I'll cover any traveling expenses."

"Well, of course! I've been only been to Germany once, and I would love to go back. When are we leaving?"

"Next week; we are going to catch the first plane to Berlin. I had already asked my brother to come over and watch Pauley. You are not busy, are you?"

"Next week, hmm, I guess I could be ready in time. And no, I have a week vacation starting next week, so I won't be needed."

"Great, that will be perfect. We'll leave here at 7:00 a.m., Monday morning. Also, I'm thinking of asking Scooter to join us. You remember him, the kid who we met a few years ago during the whole Myron tires debacle?"

"That kid who works at the auto shop? Yes, I remember him well, and as a matter of fact, I still have his phone number."

"Splendid!" said Joey, "An extra hand couldn't hurt, and he's resourceful when it comes to planning moves of action. He was tactful when he solved that tire case. He's also handy with a six-shooter, and we can buy one overseas, in case we run into trouble."

"You're right, that's a good idea. I will be there."

"Good. Talk to you later, Radford. Remember, 7:00 a.m."

"Don't ya worry; I know my time. See you tomorrow!"

****

A few days later, Joey readied his passports for the long trip to Berlin. He carefully placed them in his coat pocket and turned to the rocks.

"OK, rocks," said Joey shutting his leather suitcase, "Time we get moving."

"Guess so," agreed Ks, "We have got a long trip ahead of us."

They bounded down the stairs to the front desk to say goodbye to the two front desk ladies.

"Here's the key to our room, Miss Jane," said Joey as he handed her the key.

"Leaving again?" asked Miss Jane as she took the key.

"Where to this time?" asked Ms. Mary.

"To Ber…"

"Berlin!" exclaimed the ladies before Joey could finish.

"Yes, we are on the trail of another mystery, and Berlin is where we can hopefully find some answers." Joey replied.

"That's the furthest I believe you ever decided to travel," pondered Miss Jane.

Then she turned to the rocks. "Be sure to watch over him and bring him back home safely, alright?"

"Sure ma'am," assured Roc with a sigh, "We will."

Joey waved goodbye to the women as he lugged the heavy suitcase out the door, the rocks following close behind.

"Alrighty, rocks, to the airport," said Joey, who nodded in the direction of the airport.

Radford and Scooter were waiting outside the apartment. Detective Radford was a rather large man in his late fifties, with round glasses perched on his nose and brown fedora on of his head. Radford was a veteran detective of the New Orleans PD who had been in the field for over thirty years. Radford and Joey had been good friends for quite some time now, and they held each other in mutual respect.

Scooter was a nineteen-year-old Texan with so much hair gel rubbed through his yellow hair that it stood in spikes across his head. He had on his trademark, old faded, denim vest over a white T-shirt. While working on a confusing case a few years ago, Joey and the rocks had met Scooter at his job, an auto shop called Auto Hero. Scooter played a huge role in solving that case. Since then, Scooter was a good friend to both Joey and Radford. Radford had told Scooter everything about the ruby cat case, so Scooter was up to date.

"Hey, Scooter," Joey shook hands with both, "Good to see you again!"

"Good to see ya, Joey," replied Scooter, in his Southern slang, "Hard to believe it's already been a few months since we met."

"Yes," agreed Joey, "It seemed like only a week ago I met you at the auto garage."

"Are you ready, good chap?" asked Radford.

"Ready," replied Joey, "Time we get moving."

After loading their cases in the trunk, the five piled into Joey's black, Mercedes Benz C-Class sedan, Joey drove to the airport.

The airport was extremely busy that day. After a few minutes of searching for a parking spot, Joey parked his car and the five climbed out. They unpacked their luggage from the trunk and started their long walk to the entrance.

As soon as the group entered the airport, they headed towards the ticket counter. They had their tickets processed and made their way to board the first plane to Berlin.

In the airport, a few men, who took notice of Joey and his pals, began to murmur amongst themselves. One nodded and they followed Joey and his friends to the passenger terminal that boarded the plane. They walked by Joey, Radford, and Scooter in their seats, with their heads lowered, as if they meant to hide their faces. They sat a few rows behind Joey and his pals, appearing to watch their every move. At that moment, a flight attendant spoke up on the ceiling speakers.

"Attention ladies and gentlemen, please fasten your seatbelts. The plane is about to take off."

Everyone fastened his or her seatbelts and the plane began rolling down the runway. It then lifted off at great speed. Joey looked down at the rocks.

"Here we go, rocks," he grinned, "Berlin is a half a day away." He then thought to himself, *rubies here we come.*

Chapter 6: Berlin

The plane finally landed at the Berlin airport hours later. Joey, Radford, Scooter, and the rocks got off the airplane and headed to the terminal. Walking over to the passport registration booth, Joey Scooter, and Radford had their passports stamped. They now could travel anywhere they wanted to in Berlin. They took a train to downtown Berlin, which was only a few minutes ride away. The legend of the Ruby Cat was an old one, and since the downtown areas of cities are usually the oldest parts, Joey decided that it was a good place to start. Finding a place to start in downtown Berlin was the hard part though.

"So, what now?" asked Scooter.

"Don't know," answered Joey, "We got a lot of work ahead of us. Let's first rent a hotel for the night. It will be getting dark soon."

The group agreed and they headed off to find a hotel.

Meanwhile, the mysterious individuals who had followed Joey had their passports stamped too. They walked over to a man waiting at the airport's café. The man wore a dark brown trench coat with a fedora matching the coat. He looked to be in his fifties with smoky gray hair. The man looked up at the group approaching.

X-32

"Are those the three men you've been telling me about," asked the man.

"Sure are, Clarkson," answered one of the individuals, "followed them here from all the way back in New Orleans."

"All right," said Clarkson, "I'll contact Mr. Bernard and tell him how things are going. Remember, Bernard has paid been big money by the boss to keep them out of his hair, so we must do this right."

Clarkson turned to Frank, one of his cronies. "Follow them and see what you can find out."

Frank nodded and walked away.

****

The next morning was beautiful, with the sun just peaking over the horizon as Joey and his friends left their hotel. Joey looked around the city of Berlin and breathed in the city air. "Well," said Joey, "Time to start looking for answers."

As they walked through downtown Berlin, Ks noticed something. "Hey, Joey," he asked, "What's this line in stone on the ground for?"

"This line represents the wall that separated Communist East Germany from the free West Germany during the Cold War," replied Joey. "It was called the Berlin Wall. It was torn down in 1989, and Communist hold that separated the two countries was broken."

"Oh," said Ks, "I assume Communism is not necessarily a good thing."

"Right," answered Radford, "Communism is when the government controls what is bought and sold, jobs, what you do and shouldn't do, and where you live. All land in a Communist country is public property and each person works and is paid according to their needs and special abilities."

"Wait…" Joey pondered, "You and Roc never learned about the Berlin wall?"

"Well, we never traveled to Germany," Roc said.

"So," Scooter interrupted, "Where is this ceramic shop that made the statues?"

"Don't know," replied Joey, "It could be torn down by now."

Joey looked down the street, looking left and right. Just then, he spotted a little shop that made ceramic statues, just like the gentleman at the convention described.

"Come on," exclaimed Joey, "There is a shop up ahead that makes statues! They might know something about the history of the cat statue!"

Ks turned to Roc, "Thank goodness we are here in March instead of running around in the summer."

****

A few blocks behind, Frank ran back to the group of men standing around a streetlamp.

"Hey Clarkson," said Frank, "They are going to the little ceramics shop, the *Keramik Wiederherstellung*, down the street."

"A ceramics shop?" Clarkson rubbed his chin, "Ah, getting interesting. They obviously want to know more about the legend. Keep up with them to find out what their next steps are, but don't let them see you!"

"You got it," said Frank. He turned away and resumed his stealth mission.

****

Joey, Radford, Scooter, and the rocks stopped in front of the little shop. Joey put a hand over his eyes and peered through the front windows. The shop was empty of people except for a young boy sitting behind the front counter, polishing a ceramic vase. Joey turned to his group.

"First thing we should do is talk to the owner," said Joey, "They might have details about the Ruby Cat we are missing." He turned to Scooter and the rocks, "Could you guys watch our bags while we're inside?"

"Alrighty," said Scooter, "Good luck."

Chapter 7: The Ceramics Shop

The young boy smiled at his reflection in a shiny vase he had just finished. This piece was ready, on to the next one. Suddenly, he heard the bell ring at the front door. *Customers,* he thought. The boy's family hadn't received many visitors for a while, and it would be nice to get some business. He ran to the back room of the store and called his father.

"Father!" he exclaimed in German, "We have two customers!"

The boy's father was sitting in a chair with a newspaper in his hands. He was a tall man of average build, with bushy, brown sideburns and a mustache. Sitting next to him were his wife and his twelve-year-old daughter. Across the small room sat an elderly man and woman, the boy's grandparents, on a small soda. Only one window, facing the street, provided light for the room.

"Customers?" the man asked, "Finally, after two days of no sales!"

He hurried out to the front counter. His son and daughter followed behind. He greeted Joey and Radford, shaking their hands eagerly.

"*Guten Tag,* friends, how are you? Come and look at the beautiful items from my store! My name is Klaus Abel."

The boy walked up holding a vase, "How about this fine piece of porcelain?" He asked persuasively, "It's one of the best examples of sculpting in the city!"

The girl chimed in, "Or this one," she said. She held up a statue of a cat, a very familiar cat to Joey's. Joey and Radford were shocked! "This is one of our favorites," she continued.

"Actually, I was going to ask you about that one," Joey responded.

Mr. Klaus looked surprised. "You were?" he asked.

"Yes," answered Joey, "Do you know anything about two rubies that were stashed in a statue just like that one? It's an old legend we've been following."

Mr. Klaus wrinkled an eyebrow and stroked his chin, "A cat with rubies in it you say? Nothing comes to my knowledge; how much do you know about this matter?"

"Only half the story," said Joey, "We know that statue shop that produced these cat statues was in Berlin, so we started our search here."

"Grandpa told us about that story once," the boy spoke up, "It was a few years ago, but I remember some of it now."

"Wait, I can introduce you to my father," Mr. Klaus added, "He's in the back room."

"Alright, thank you," said Joey, "We'd be delighted to hear what he has to say."

Mr. Klaus nodded and led Joey and Radford around the counter towards the rear of the shop. He waved his hand to his parents and wife and introduced them to Radford and Joey.

"This is my wife, Maria, and these are my parents, *Herr und Frau Abel*" he said. He then spoke to his father, "These men want to know about a statue that holds… rubies inside."

The grandfather sat up straight in his chair to stare Radford and Joey in the eyes. He cleared his throat.

"The Ruby Cat has a curse on it," he said in a raspy tone, "You should stay away from it."

"A curse," Radford said and looked at Joey, "Joey here didn't say anything about a curse."

"I didn't think it was such a big deal," Joey shrugged, "Thought it was just a made-up story."

"Ah, *es ist am wahrsten*," the grandfather laughed and tapped his cane on the floor, "*It is most true*, but it isn't widely known. Let me tell you it's story and you will see how real the curse is! Sixty years ago, there was this couple from South Korea named Mr. and Mrs. Narong; they had learned about the legend of the jewels hidden in a plaster cat. They thought they could make a fortune! It was no easy task, but eventually they found a statue which they believed to be the Ruby Cat. *Ach*, they were not the only ones who had their eyes on it! Mr. Narong was out that day and when he came back, *ach*, he found his poor wife dead from a gun wound in their apartment! The police proved that a gang of thugs had broken in and killed her to steal the cat statue. It was not but a few days later that Mr. Narong had died in a hospital from a severe case of pneumonia. So let me tell you, the curse is real!"

The family was stunned after this horrifying tale. Joey and Radford looked at each other, bewildered. Never had they heard about these events, they had been swept under the rug of history, just like the legend of the Ruby Cat itself.

"Well, do you know where we could find the shop," Joey asked, trying to change the subject, "The shop that made the plaster cats to begin with?"

"That's been long torn down by now," the grandfather replied, "You will not find it."

"Is there anything else you could tell us that could help in our search?" Radford asked, "We could use advice on where to…"

"No, no more!" the grandfather roared, "The curse is real, and we can't… no, we *won't* help you!"

Radford tried asking again, "But if you could give us even the smallest hint on where to start…"

"It would bring the curse upon us and our home!" exclaimed the mother, "Never!"

"It's fine," Joey said reassuringly, holding up his hand, "We aren't concerned about the myths, we just need to…"

"How could you even be sure we won't be affected by the curse," the grandmother chimed in, "That's it, you can't! You don't have any way to prove it won't!"

"No, sorry, sirs," Mr. Klaus interrupted, "Like my family has said, we won't help you."

Joey stood silent with his hand still raised.

"It's known to attack everyone and anyone who dare look for the statue!" the grandfather said, "It's too much of a risk for any of us!"

"We aren't asking you to join us in our quest, my good man," Radford continued, "We just need to know where to start. Besides, giving us a that bit of information shouldn't affect you in any way; curses or gangs."

The family was quiet for a bit, and then began to murmur among themselves. After a few seconds, they looked up at Radford and Joey.

"Alright, sirs," Mr. Klaus said at last, "I guess it wouldn't hurt us to just *tell* you where to look. You might find some answers at the *Zentral- und Landesbibliothek Berlin*; the *Berliner Stadtbibliothek*, two blocks down the street. Though, whatever you do, please be careful. You have our blessing."

"Thank you," said Joey, shaking the father's hand "*Auf Wiedersehen*, sir."

He and Radford left the back room. As they were heading to the front door, the boy and girl ran to Joey and tugged on his arm.

"Sir, take this," they said excitedly handing him a small token, "It will keep you safe in danger."

"Oh?" replied Joey in awe, "Thank you...?"

Joey opened his hand to look at the token. It was a round disk with a four-leaf clover in the middle. A good luck charm? Joey was confused. Not knowing what else

to do, he put the token in his coat pocket and caught up to Radford as they exited the shop.

"Well?" asked Roc, walking up to them, "What did you find?"

"Not much," replied Radford, "Obviously they are afraid of the curse Joey didn't tell me about"

"They told us to look at the *Zentral-* und *Landesbi*…the *Landesbi*…" Joey gave up trying to pronounce the long words halfway through. "The Berlin Library," he finally stated, "They told us to go to the Berlin Library two blocks down the street from here."

"Okay, let's go then. I'm bored standing around here," complained Scooter.

Joey, Radford, Scooter, and the rocks arrived at the library fifteen minutes later. Joey left the others outside resting on a bench and entered the building. He began his search on one of the public computers for any books that might have information about the Ruby Cat.

"405.2 – 405.23," Joey said to himself "Bingo."

As he walked over to the aisles that held the books, he heard voices coming from its middle section.

"Here it is," exclaimed a voice in a loud whisper. "It's the book about the Ruby Cat!"

Ruby Cat!? Joey said to himself.

"Yes," said another voice, "now we will find the rubies!"

Joey peered around the aisle to see two young men, flipping through a book.

"I hope no one else knows about this," said one boy, "Don't want to attract attention."

"Yes," said the other, "Who's knows what they would do to get their hands on the rubies."

More than you can imagine, thought Joey.

"May I help you?"

Joey spun around to see a librarian smiling behind him. He looked back at the young men and found them staring at him, suspiciously.

"Uh, no, I'm fine, thank you," he said as he turned back into the other aisle.

Spigots, thought Joey, *she blew my cover.* He decided to leave the aisle before any trouble happened. He glanced back quickly to see the young men looking at their book again. *Good,* he thought, quickly walking back to the computer. He checked one more time just to see if there were any more books about the Ruby Cat.

****

Meanwhile, Bert and Alice, the children from the shop, had followed Joey, Radford, Scooter, and the rocks to the library. They were holding a statue, but not just any statue; it was a grey cat statue very similar to the Ruby Cat.

"They really shouldn't be getting in that mess," said Alice to Bert, "They should stop looking for the Ruby Cat."

He looked at her, "I know you're concerned, Alice. I am, too. We need to show them this statue first, though."

"Still, I wish they would leave the whole business alone."

The kids were nearly at the library. The only thing separating them from the library was an alley. Suddenly, Clarkson and two of his men jumped out of the alley. One grabbed the statue Bert was holding!

"Give me that back!" shouted Bert. He struggled to keep a hold of the statue, but the man had a firm grasp.

"Get the statue and let's go!" shouted Clarkson.

With a mighty yank, the man pulled the statue out of Bert's hands.

As if planned, a third man in a black Chrysler pulled up to where they were.

"Get in!" he shouted to the man with the statue.

Alice looked back and forth, panicking. Just then, she saw Scooter, Radford, and the rocks waiting on a bench outside the library.

"Sirs," Alice shouted, "Help us!"

Scooter, Radford, and the rocks saw the kids struggling with the men.

"Don't worry! We're coming!" shouted Radford, running towards them.

Clarkson turned around to see the four charging their way. "Confound it," he muttered under his breath, "Trouble."

****

Inside the library, Joey was still lingering around the aisles. Suddenly, he heard screaming and shouting outside. He ran out of the aisles and saw people in the library pointing out of a window. He ran to the window to look out. There was a group of people fighting by a black car in the street. It was Radford and Scooter! Joey burst out of the library and shot down the sidewalk towards the brawl.

****

Scooter ran with a burst of speed toward the first man and struck him in the jaw. The crook fell over onto the pavement, dropping the Ruby Cat.

"Stop them!" yelled Clarkson.

The second man from the gang stepped in front of Scooter.

"Alright, boy," he muttered, "This isn't any of your business.

The thug threw a side punch to Scooter's face. Scooter ducked to the left, and kicked the villain's leg, causing him to fall.

The first crook got off the ground, rubbing his chin. He stepped up behind Scooter and was about to give him a blow to the head with a nightstick.

"Hey," yelled Roc, "Hold your horses, man!"

Roc jumped up to hit the man's stomach. The man fell to the ground, huffing. He began to rise again, but Ks jumped on the guy and gave him a punch to the nose. The man fell flat on the pavement.

"Too easy," Ks laughed.

However, Ks spoke too soon. The third big, burly thug climbed out of the car and snorted. He started walking towards the rocks.

"Uh oh," said Roc, "Looks like he's trouble. Not!"

Roc jumped at the mass of muscle, but the thug caught Roc like he was basketball. Ks jumped at the man too, but he grabbed Ks in the same manner.

"Rats," muttered Ks.

The crook swung them around and around and threw them into a café window.

Crash!!!

Two people at the table screamed as the rocks landed on their donuts and coffee. Others in the café jumped up from their tables and ran out the door.

"Heh," chuckled the thug.

The first man climbed to his feet again and pointed his gun at Scooter. Scooter swung his arm in a quick side strike motion and knocked the gun out of the man's hand. Scooter snatched it up off the sidewalk.

"Hands up!" he yelled to everyone, "Nobody move!"

Everyone froze, and the crooks put their hands in the air, except Clarkson. He crept around the back of the car with a club and snuck up behind Scooter.

"Look out!" shouted Radford.

Clarkson struck down hard on Scooter's back with the club. Scooter staggered and fell, dropping the gun. Clarkson picked up the gun and pointed it at Radford and Scooter.

"You two stay back," he scowled, "these kids have a possible Ruby Cat and we're taking it."

Joey burst into view and saw the men getting in the car. The men turned and spotted Joey coming towards them. Clarkson backed towards the car and shouted, "Get him off our tail!"

The men fired several rounds at Joey. Joey dove to the ground as the bullets flew over him. The four crooks scrambled into the car and drove away. Joey picked himself up and watched the car speed out of view. He hurried over to Radford, Scooter, and the kids to see how they were. Scooter was sitting on the ground, rubbing his back.

"Are you all alright?" Joey asked.

"Yes," Radford replied, "We're all fine."

"Speak for yourself," grumbled Scooter, "Ouch."

"What did they take?" Joey asked again.

"We had a cat statue in our family for generations," replied Bert, "We were bringing it to show it to you, but those crooks took it.

"We'll track them down," reassured Joey, "Don't you worry."

He turned to Radford and Scooter, "Go back to our hotel to get the rest of our belongings. Call the German police and tell them to be the lookout for a 1981, black,

Chrysler New Yorker. I managed to see the license plate number…RA-KL 8136."

"Right!" said Radford, and he and Scooter took off for the hotel.

At that moment, Joey heard a clinking noise. He looked around and saw the rocks swaying towards them. They were covered in donut crumbs and coffee.

"Rocks!" he exclaimed, "What happened?"

"One of those dudes threw us into the café," answered Roc.

"Where's Radford and Scooter?" asked Ks.

"They went back to the hotel to gather our things," replied Joey, "We are going to follow those men back to wherever they are hiding out at."

"Okay," said Roc, "we'll help them pack."

With that, the rocks wobbled off towards the hotel. Bert and Alice just stared at the rocks.

"Where did you find those stones?" said Bert, scratching his head.

"Did a witch give those to you?" Alice asked.

Joey chuckled, "I don't know where they came from…they found me when I was a young kid. Now, you two had better run home. Your parents will be wondering where you are."

"Alright," replied Bert.

Bert and Alice headed back to their shop and Joey hurried on to the hotel.

Chapter 8: Tracking

Joey and the group woke early the next morning. After getting themselves ready for the day, they waited for a call from the police in the living room area of their hotel suite. Scooter read a travel brochure while Radford looked through the newspaper. Joey paced back and forth through the living room. The air was tense and quiet as they waited; that is, until Roc and Ks exploded into the room, wearing aprons and chef hats.

"Breakfast is ready!" they shouted.

The three jumped. Radford's glasses fell off his face onto the floor while Scooter clutched his chest.

"Don't scare us like that," exclaimed Scooter, "My heart's jumpin'!"

"Oh, sorry!" said the rocks in unison, "We ran out of eggs and bacon, so we had to fix some Lunchables."

"Oh, wow," Scooter said unenthusiastically, "Delicious."

"Hurry up and eat," the rocks hollered, "Or it will get cold!"

Joey, Radford, and Scooter froze at the thought of cooked Lunchables for breakfast.

"Are they supposed to be heated up?" Scooter asked.

Joey shrugged, "They can be, but they are usually eaten at lunch, not breakfast."

"I was really looking forward to bacon and eggs," mumbled Radford, "Not microwaved pizza."

The three bravely entered the kitchen to consume the warm meals.

After the unpleasant breakfast, there still was no call, and the group was growing restless. They knew if they didn't get a call soon, the crooks would be out of the city and long gone.

"If things don't pick up the pace," said Radford, "We might as well say 'Goodbye rubies.'"

"I know," replied Joey, "I really hope the police find them. Time is running out."

Like an answer to their complaints, the phone rang. Joey quickly answered. "Hello, Joey Packard speaking."

"Gutnen Morgan, Mr. Packard, this is Officer Schneider of the Berlin Police, the car that you described to us has just been sighted."

"Brilliant! Where's the location?"

"The car is located at Berlin Central Station. A caller told us that a black Chrysler with the same license plate was parked outside of the station."

"Thanks, we'll be right there!"

Joey quickly hung up the phone and grabbed his trench coat.

"Well," demanded Ks, "Where are they?"

"To the Berlin Central Station!" Joey answered, flinging the coat over his shoulder as they headed out of the room.

****

"Are you sure it was the car, Officer?" Joey asked the police officer. They had arrived at Central Station, a massive glass cathedral, only a few minutes before.

"Positive," said the officer, "just like the description you gave us."

"Good," replied Joey as he turned to Radford. "You, Scooter and the rocks stay here. Keep an eye on the clock so we don't miss our train. I'm going with Officer Schneider to check out the car."

Outside the station, another officer guarded the black Chrysler parked in the train station's parking lot. Joey and Officer Schneider pushed through the crowds towards the car. Joey looked the car over.

"Yes, this is the car!" He asked the officer guarding the car, "Did you find anything important on it, something that could give us a lead as to where they are headed?"

"No, it's empty," replied the officer, "look for yourself."

The officer opened the car door and Joey looked inside. *Just need one clue to give us a hint,* he said to himself. He leaned inside to get a look at the dashboard. Empty. He opened the glove compartment, but nothing was in it either. Joey stopped to think, *the car seats, what if I looked between the car seats?* He ran his hand through the cracks of the front seats. Not much was in them, only a few gum wrappers. He crawled into the back seats and searched them. A piece of paper in the left side of the seat caught his eye. He pulled out the paper to read it, and then he

froze. It was a train ticket! He scrambled out of the car and held the ticket in front of the police.

"Here!" he exclaimed, "I found this ticket…The men must have dropped it. Look at its destination, London. If we take that train, we should find our crooks."

"Ah," said Officer Schneider, "Nice observation!"

"Thanks for your help, officers," said Joey as he shook the officers' hand, "We need to catch the train before it leaves."

"Alright," boomed Officer Schneider, "Good luck!"

Joey ran back into the train station and found Radford, Scooter, and the rocks idling about.

"Did you find anything?" asked Scooter, chugging a cola.

"Sure did," answered Joey, "Look at this. This ticket is for the train headed to London. I found it in the crevasse of the back seats. The train leaves in five minutes; if we hurry, we can make it on time."

They grabbed their bags and headed towards the ticket counter. After buying their tickets, the group hastily made their way to the train. The conductor was about to blow his whistle, but the group burst into view just before he could give the engineer the "all clear" sign. A few minutes later and the five would've been stuck waiting for another train.

After jumping on the train, they found their seats on the first car. Joey cautiously looked around the car, making sure they were out of sight from the statue thieves.

To his relief, the thieves weren't in this car. He turned to the others.

"I'm going to wash up," he told them, "And while I'm at it, I am going to search the other cars for those crooks."

"Alright," whispered Radford, nodding his head, "Be careful."

Joey left his seat and headed for the washroom in the last car, glancing at the passengers as he walked by. He passed through all nine cars, but no one matched the men's features. Upon leaving the washroom, he headed back to his seat. As he was walking through the eighth car, he dropped his watch he was putting back on his wrist. It fell near the feet of a man reading a newspaper.

"Hey, young man," he said, without looking up from his paper, "You dropped something."

"Oh, thanks," replied Joey.

As he bent down to pick it up, he looked at the man reading. He froze. It was the man with the fedora! Joey glanced at the other seats. The other three crooks were sleeping in the seats beside the man! He slowly picked his watch up and walked away, not looking back. He hoped the man didn't recognize him, or they would all be in trouble. He made it back to the first car and plumped in his seat. He turned to his friends.

"They are on this train," he whispered.

"Did they see you?" Roc whispered back.

"No," replied Joey, "I don't think so…"

✱✱✱✱✱✱✱✱✱✱✱✱✱✱✱✱✱✱

The train arrived in Cologne, Germany at three o'clock in the afternoon. Joey looked through a map to track their remaining route.

"We got another stop in Brussels, Belgium before London," he said.

"How many more hours will it take?" yawned Scooter.

"It will take another two hours to get to Brussels," replied Joey, "and another two to three hours from Brussels to London."

"Whew!" whistled Ks, "we go a long trip ahead of us. What do these guys want in London anyway?"

"Not sure," answered Joey, "Anyway, let's go get something to eat before the train leaves again."

"Great!" exclaimed Radford, "Let's go to Petere's Brauhaus. I've been there once on a vacation, and they have excellent food."

"Sounds good," replied Joey, "Let's hurry, the train leaves in an hour. Also, keep an eye out for our thieving friends. We don't want to be seen."

After some delicious bratwurst and plum dumplings at Petere's, they made their way back to the station. Finding their seats, they sat down just as the train whistle roared. Joey looked around the car.

"I'm going to check if they are still on this train," he told the others, "Gotta make sure they are here before the train leaves."

"Good idea," said Radford, wiping his glasses.

Joey left his seat and advanced to the car that the crooks were sitting in. He peered through the window on the door that separated the cars. Sure enough, they were in the same seats. *Good,* thought Joey. He made it back to his seat and sat down with a sigh. The train slowly began rolling out of the station. Joey decided to take a nap before the next station's arrival.

****

WHHHEEEEEEUUUUUWWWW!!!!!

Joey jerked out of his sleep. The train whistle meant they were at the Brussels's station. He checked his watch which read 5:30p.m.

"Time to stretch our legs," he yawned while standing up, "there's an hour wait for the next train."

"Alright," said Scooter, "What will we do in the meantime?"

"We can tour Brussels's Central Square," replied Joey, "If you're up to it."

"Sure!" exclaimed Radford, "It's time we get some fresh air."

The five stepped off the train after receiving their luggage and walked down the platform of the station. Suddenly, Joey shoved Radford and Scooter into the crowd leaving the train. Ks and Roc were puzzled but followed them into the crowd. Radford and Scooter were speechless.

"What was that for?" exclaimed Radford, crossly.

"Shhh!" whispered Joey; he pointed to the end of the platform, "The thieves are walking on the platform too, and they almost spotted us."

"My word," gasped Radford as they watched the men.

They mingled with the crowd until the crooks passed by. The crooks didn't seem to notice them, however. The group breathed a sigh of relief.

A few minutes passed as they strolled to Brussels's Grand Place. Holding a travel guide, Joey pointed out the city's different attractions. Just then, Ks shouted in delight.

"Look!" cried Ks, "it's the La Boutique Tintin! The Tintin shop! He is our favorite comic book hero! We must buy something!" Without waiting for a second thought, Ks ran off towards the store.

"Don't worry, Joey," Roc grinned, following Ks, "I'll make sure he doesn't shop long. And I'll make sure he doesn't give the store owner a heart attack!"

Ten minutes later, they came out with a bag full of Tintin comics, hats, and figurines.

"Okay," said Ks, throwing a Tintin cap on his head, "Ready!"

As they continued roaming around Brussels's Town Square, they spotted a familiar shop. Radford perked up at the sight of it.

"Starbucks!" he exclaimed, "A taste of home!"

Radford briskly walked into the shop with Scooter following behind. They came out shortly after with coffee and donut holes. Radford enthusiastically handed a steaming mocha coffee to Joey.

"Uh, thanks, Radford," said Joey, taking the cup, even though he wasn't a big coffee drinker.

After touring The Grand Place a bit more, it was time for them to board the train. Just as they were walking to the train, Joey stopped in his tracks. He spotted the crooks once again waiting in line for the train.

"Look!" he whispered, "They're splitting up!"

The four men were huddled in a circle, whispering to each other. The man in the fedora nodded to everyone as they left and headed to the train bound for London. He held a suitcase in hand. The three men walked in a different direction towards another train.

"Crumpets!" exclaimed Roc, "what do we do now?"

"We're splitting up," said Joey, "The rocks and I will follow the man in the fedora to London. You two follow the men wherever they go. Whatever you do, be careful."

"Sure thing," agreed Scooter, and with that, he and Radford headed to the new train.

Joey breathed in deep, "Okay Ks, Roc, let's not lose him. We've come too far to mess this up."

He picked up his suitcase to follow the man. The chase had resumed. Joey knew one thing for sure; this trip was going to be a whole lot more than a simple treasure hunt.

Chapter 9: Operation Ruby Cat

The sun was warm, the seagulls were singing. A hammock hung from a palm tree, and a small table was beside it. Set upon the table was a pina colada. Scooter picked it up, took a long drink, and then slammed it back onto the table. He tucked into the hammock. Ahhh! It was wonderful here at the beach. He was ready to take a nap. Wait . . . for some reason his tree started swaying. He was swinging back and forth; a strong wind seemed to be blowing. Then, a voice boomed from the sky.

"Scooter, Scooter!" said Radford, as he nudged him out of his sleep. "We are in France, at the Gare Du Nord station. The men chose to come here for some reason."

Scooter woke up. The palm trees disappeared; the hammock was gone. The seagulls were nowhere to be seen. Scooter sighed; what a wonderful dream it was. Radford picked up his bag and got off his seat. He whispered to Scooter.

"Keep an eye on those crooks," he said pointing a finger, "We don't want to be seen, since you and I were the first ones they encountered."

"Yeah, I get it," mumbled Scooter, rubbing his eyes.

While leaving the train, Radford bought two newspapers from a stand. He handed one to Scooter and motioned him to sit down on a bench and read.

The Gare Du Nord was an insanely massive train station, shaped exactly like an old cathedral. Several trains could fit side by side in its passenger boarding bay.

Radford leaned over to Scooter, "Perfect plan, eh?"

"Huh?" asked Scooter, "We're reading newspapers as the thieves get away. I don't see that as a good plan."

"Correct!" winked Radford, "As the crooks go by, we can spy on them and follow them."

"Ah," Scooter beamed, "I see now."

Peering over the papers, they scanned the crowds trying to pinpoint out the three men. Radford turned his head this way and that, hoping it wasn't too late.

He spotted a Starbucks and stared. A cup of coffee would be wonderful now! There was a line though; three men were waiting for their drinks. *Hold on,* he thought, *those three men! They're the crooks!* He nudged Scooter in the elbow and pointed to the coffee shop.

"There!" he whispered, "They're at Starbucks."

"Let's go get us some coffee!" grinned Scooter.

"I've got the perfect idea how to get close," said Radford, "And this time it's not newspapers."

Getting off the seat, they threw down their papers and headed to Starbucks. Radford took disguises out of his bag and handed them to Scooter, who reluctantly put them on. A pair of shades, baseball hats, and fake beards was all it took to get close. Entering the shop, Radford slapped down a few bills on the counter.

"Two large cups of 100% black coffee," he said in a deeper tone, "and hold the cream and sugar."

The worker raised an eyebrow but didn't say a word. He poured the drinks and handed them to the strange customers. Radford and Scooter sat down at a table a few feet behind the three men. They drank their coffee, listening intently to the crooks' plan.

"So, have you seen anybody followin' us, Bill?" the first thug asked the second man. He had a strong western American accent.

"Nope," said Bill, the massive thug, "None that I recall."

"Good," replied the first thug, whose name was Stan. He looked over to the third man, "And you, Frank?"

"Haven't seen a thing since we left them folk in Berlin," replied Frank.

"Excellent," said Stan, "Now we can get to our destination without worrying about looking behind our backs wherever we go. Okay, these are the plans. Mr. Bernard wants us to meet one of his people in Paris. A few rumors have pointed to the real Ruby Cat being there. Of course, the chance is very small."

"Oh, come on!" boomed Bill, "Honestly, what are we doing here in Paris just because of some gossip? The statues were shipped to America, not France! For that matter, why don't we just go to Sweden, or Norway, for goodness' sake, and follow all the rumors there!?"

"We must take every lead we can," responded Stan, "The rumors are from pretty reliable sources, but one can never be too sure. That's why we are taking the risk. Besides, Mr. Bernard is just taking orders from the big man himself."

"Okay," Bill grumbled, "We better get paid well for this."

Getting off their seats, the men exited the café. Radford and Scooter looked at each other.

"Well," said Radford, "We know their boss's name is Mr. Bernard, and we know where they are going. We got to keep up with them."

"I wonder where they are hiding the Ruby Cat they stole from those kids back in Berlin?" pondered Scooter.

"That guy in the fedora must have it," said Radford, snapping his fingers, "Luckily, Joey is after him."

"Right," said Scooter, gulping down the last of his coffee.

They left the shop in a hurry to catch up with the three men, keeping as much distance between them as possible. Seeing the crooks leave the station and board a bus to downtown Paris, they did so too, with haste. They tailed the men onto the bus and looked for their seats. While doing so, Scooter accidentally bumped into someone.

"Hey, watch it, bud!" exclaimed the man.

Scooter froze. The man was one of the thieves. He stared at Scooter. Scooter regained his senses and straightened his shoulders.

"Uh, sorry, sir," he said and was about to walk away to his seat, but the man grabbed him by the shoulder.

"Wait a minute," he said, "You look familiar…"

****

Joey felt a little knob bumping his right arm as he awoke. Roc and Ks were trying to rouse him from his slumber.

"The train has stopped," said Roc, "We are in London."

Joey stood and stretched, "Alright," he grunted, rubbing his eyes, "Why, this guy is running everywhere! Oh well, let's hit the trail again."

Grabbing his bag, Joey and the rocks left the train. He stepped behind a food cart and watched the man as he walked through the crowds. Joey slowly followed him, keeping his distance so he wouldn't be seen. The man left the station and headed down the streets of London, Joey and the rocks trailing behind. They had walked for a few blocks when the man stopped near a light pole. Joey and the rocks hid themselves behind a phone booth. The man lit a cigar and seemed to be waiting for someone. Joey counted the time on his watch; five minutes had passed. Suddenly, a red SUV pulled up next to the curb where the man was waiting. The person in the car rolled down the window. Joey squinted closely and made out that it was a woman in the front seat. They seemed to have started a conversation. He peered through the glass of the phone booth and watched, quietly. Joey could now get a good look at the man. He had a chin full of scruff with dark, brown eyebrows and a forehead creased with wrinkles. The man scowled at anybody who walked by.

"Morning, Love!" said the woman in a British accent, "Where to?"

"To Mr. Bernard's place," the man responded, "and, please, quit calling me *Love.*"

"Sure thing, Love," the woman responded.

The man sighed and got into the car. The woman put the car in drive and rolled away. Joey quickly ran into the road, keeping an eye on the car. He took out his SD and snapped a picture of the plate's number before the car drove out of sight. He turned to the rocks; they both were still behind the phone booth.

"Rocks, find a taxi, quick!"

Roc and Ks left the phone booth and ran down the street. Spotting a taxi on the other side of the street, they ran after it and knocked on the door. A man opened the door and jumped upon seeing two rocks near his car.

"Hurry!" said Roc, pointing to the red car, "We need you to follow that red SUV!"

"Right, mate!" said the man, who was still puzzled at seeing talking rocks.

"First," said Roc, "we need to wait for our friend over there."

Ks turned and called Joey. Joey came running up to the car, clambered in, and slammed the door.

"Okay, driver," he said, "We're ready!"

The driver cranked the engine and sped away. He looked in the rear-view mirror at Joey.

"These rocks are yours, mate?"

"Yes sir," replied Joey.

"Strange," said the driver, scratching his head.

Suddenly, unexpectedly, the driver stomped on the brakes. Joey and the rocks lunged forward with a jerk.

"Sorry, sir," apologized the driver, "A red light."

The light took at least a minute to change, and by time the traffic passed, the SUV was nowhere in sight. The driver turned to Joey and shrugged.

"What now, mate?" he asked.

"It's not a problem, sir," replied Joey, paid the cab fare, "I took a picture of the license plate before we called you. If we hurry to the police in time, they can look up the number and give us their address."

"Alrighty then," said the driver, "Good luck!"

Joey shook his hand and he and the rocks jumped out of the car and started trotting down the street. Joey pulled out his phone to find the police station nearest to them. After finding it, they proceeded to the West End Central Police Station. At the reception desk, Joey told the receptionist everything that had happened to him and read the number aloud from the photo he had taken.

"That's the number from the car. I need you to find the address of this number," Joey told the officer behind the desk, "It was a 2020, red Cadillac Escalade."

"Very well, sir," said the officer in a thick British accent, "name?"

"Joey Packard."

"Alrighty…"

After a few minutes of the officer typing on the computer, she handed Joey a paper with the address. Joey read the paper over, out loud.

"10th Downing Street, LONDON, SW1A 2AB. Thanks, ma'am."

"You're welcome, sir. An officer will go with you."

Joey nodded. An officer led him and the rocks to his patrol car, and they drove through the city to find the address. In a few minutes, they had arrived. It was a recently refurbished, medieval styled mansion. As expected, the red Cadillac was in the front driveway.

"That's the SUV," Joey told the officer.

"Right, sir," the officer said, "It's time to have a chat with our friends here."

The officer pulled up in the mansion's round driveway. At least a dozen luxury model cars were lined up in the driveway. Joey and the officer got out of the car and made their way up to the two large, black doors. There were two white domes built into each side of the building. A row of bushes spotted with flowers lined the round driveway. Joey and the officer stood at the front door as the officer rang the service bell. After a few moments, a butler answered the door.

"Good day, sir," he said in a modest fashion, "How may I help you?"

"Good day," the officer replied, "May we speak with the owner of the house?"

"I'm sorry, but he's terribly busy at the moment."

"Ah, tell him this won't take but a minute."

"Very well, sir."

The butler retreated into the house. Joey could see through the open doors that many people were hanging out in the house. A few minutes later, the butler returned with a man. The man looked like a person of high class, very well dressed. in a blue suit with silver cuff links.

"Good day, what can I do for you gentlemen?" he asked.

"Hello, sir," the officer replied and waved a hand towards Joey, "This young man believes the red Cadillac in your driveway matches the description used by somebody who stole one of his belongings."

"I'm sorry, but he's mistaken sir," the man responded, "this car never left the driveway today."

"All day," Joey said, "but how come I just saw it driving down the streets half an hour ago?"

"You must have seen a different one," the man shrugged, "check the license plate, it's different most likely."

The officer walked to the back of the SUV and checked the plate's number. He squinted at the plate in the bright sun, but he could see clearly that it was a completely different number. He walked back to the mansion's front door.

"He's right, Mr. Packard," he said, "It's not the right number."

"That's right, like I said," the man said, "It's a 2019 model. Gentlemen, if you will excuse me, I have guests I need to return to."

"Sorry for the trouble sir," the officer said, tipping the brim of his hat.

The man nodded and walked back through and shut them with a loud thud. Joey and the officer walked back to the patrol car. Joey took one last look at the SUV, nodding to himself. The rocks hopped out of the patrol car and ran up to Joey and the officer.

"Well," Ks asked, "Aren't we gonna do a full investigation?"

"No, Ks, we can't," Joey replied, "This isn't the right car."

Roc nudged Ks and muttered, "This has a feeling of deja vu to it."

"I'm sorry you didn't find the right car, Mr. Packard," the officer said, "but there isn't much more I can do."

"It's alright, officer," Joey reassured him, "thanks for your help."

The officer nodded, "Need a ride back?"

"No," Joey replied, "We can manage from here."

The officer climbed back into his car. Joey and the rocks watched as the patrol car drove out of sight. Joey turned to Ks and Roc.

"There's no way we are getting in there," he told them, "I doubt it's open to the public."

"But didn't you just say this is the wrong place?" Roc asked in bewilderment.

"It is the right vehicle," Joey said, "the SUV we followed had a scuff above its right wheel. And look, this SUV has the same."

"Why didn't you tell the officer that?" Ks asked.

"It wouldn't help much," Joey answered, "wouldn't be enough evidence to prove it's the same car. But this is the car, and the owners switched the plates and lied about the year model."

"Well then," questioned Ks, "How do we get the statue back? This place is probably swarming with security guards inside."

"There's only one thing we can do," said Joey, "If you can't sneak past the enemy, be the enemy."

A door slam brought Joey's attention to the house. A cab driver was outside with his cab, a silver 1950, Crysler New Yorker, waiting for the people inside the mansion. Joey saw the opportunity ripe for the picking. He ran up to and ducked behind the car, slowly creeping up on the driver. The driver ignorantly took a swig from his water bottle. Wait . . . did he hear footsteps? He turned to the noise and saw a fist. *Whomp!* He fell to the ground, out cold. Joey took his coat and hat and put them on. He nipped the driver's shades as well. Ks and Roc dragged the unconscious driver deep into the bushes out of sight.

"Okay, rocks," said Joey, adjusting the shades on his face, "We're in. You two hide yourselves. I'm going to go in and try to find the suitcase."

The rocks nodded and ran into the bushes. Joey took a deep breath and entered the mansion. A bell rang as he opened the door; people turned their heads towards him. Seeing he was only the driver, they paid little attention. Joey took advantage of the situation and began searching the mansion for the bag. Striding down the long halls of the mansion, Joey scanned each room with precision.

There seemed to be a party going on here, making it a little more difficult to find the man he was looking for. After searching for a few more minutes, he turned his eye and spotted the man in the fedora sitting in an armchair. He was in the guest room with a few other men sitting on fancy armchairs as well. They were deep in conversation, and Joey managed to catch the end of it. The man with the blue coat, who answered the door, spoke to the man in the fedora.

"Well, Clarkson, have you been... let me say, interrupted in your travels?"

Clarkson, Joey thought to himself. *That is the man's name.*

"None, Mr. Bernard," replied Clarkson, "Although, in Berlin, we encountered a few guys trying to ruin our plans, but we stopped them. I haven't seen their faces after that."

"Good, good!" said Mr. Bernard, "It is odd though that the boss wants to turn that mansion into a museum."

"But I fear, sir," said Clarkson, "That we will see the strangers again. They seem to be very persistent."

"Then," he sighed, "We'll just take more drastic measures. Remember, we can't fail the Boss."

Joey entered the room and cleared his throat. The men turned to him.

"I'll take your bags to the car, sir," he said, disguising his voice with a deeper tone, "When you're ready."

"Ah, good, Parker," said Clarkson, "Here's the case." He handed Joey a large leather valise.

Joey took the valise and swiftly exited the mansion. He got the keys out of the driver's coat pocket and opened the car. He turned to the hedge the rocks concealed themselves in.

"Rocks!" he exclaimed, "I got the case!"

"Awesome!" cheered the rocks as they exploded out of the bushes, "Let's get out of here!"

They hopped into the car and sped away from the mansion.

Meanwhile, the driver came to his senses. He crawled out of the bushes and rubbed his head. He looked around for the car. It was gone.

He burst into the mansion. Everyone stared at him.

"Where is the cab!?" he exclaimed.

Mr. Bernard, Clarkson, and the other men came into the lobby.

"The cab," Mr. Bernard asked, "didn't you just take the suitcase to the cab?"

"Parker," Clarkson chimed in, "What happened? Where's your uniform?"

"I don't know," replied Parker, "Some guy knocked me out and took my uniform. He apparently tricked you all and stole the cab!"

"Of all the fools," Clarkson stuttered in dread, "I just gave the suitcase with the statue to him!"

"It must have been that same guy who came here with the police!" Mr. Bernard pointed out.

"That's it, play time's over!" Clarkson turned to Parker, "Parker, call the boys, we are going to put an end to this once and for all!"

"Right away, sir," said Parker, and he ran to the upper rooms of the mansion.

Clarkson pulled out his keys and headed to a gun cabinet in a small study off of the lobby. He unlocked the case and pulled out three AK 47s. He took out a few magazines and stuffed them with 7.62x39mm rounds. These guns were now ready for some serious firing. Parker came running back down the stairs with three other men following him. Clarkson handed off the guns to the three thugs. Then both he and Parker pulled out their 9mm handgun from inside their coats.

"Alright, boys," Clarkson shouted, "Get in the van! We got some rats to catch!"

The three men threw the guns over their shoulders and ran to the van. The three men scrambled into the back of vehicle while Parker and Clarkson got in the front. Parker cranked the engine and punched the pedal. They squealed out of the driveway, in hot pursuit of the cab.

****

"By George!" exclaimed Stan. He patted Scooter on the shoulder. "Is that you, Steve? We haven't seen you in a long time, man!"

Scooter was stunned! Apparently, his disguise made him appear to be an old friend of these men. He decided to play along with the act.

"Uh, yeah," he said in a low voice, "It's great to see you again!"

The men looked at Radford. "Who's your friend here?" asked Frank.

"Ah, gentlemen," said Scooter, patting Radford on the back, "This here is my good ol' pal, Allen. We go back a long way."

"Splendid!" Stan exclaimed, shaking Radford's hand, "Any friend of yours is a friend of ours!"

"Nice to meet you, gentlemen," Radford replied, meekly.

"So, what are you three doing today?" Scooter asked.

"We've been sent on an errand by our man at the mansion, Mr. Bernard," Stan told them, "It's top secret, so we can't tell you."

"Exciting," Scooter grinned, "May we join you?"

"Nah," Stan laughed, "No offense, I can't bring you along. Now, don't get me wrong, I would like to take you with us, but I don't think the boss would allow it."

"No problem," replied Scooter, "We understand. Besides, we have places to go."

"Alright," Stan said, patting Scooter on the back, "See ya around, dude."

"See ya later," Scooter said, and he and Radford shook the men's hands.

The three walked away to their seats, and Scooter and Radford returned to theirs. Radford plumped down on the seat.

"That was a close one!" he said, wiping his brow with his handkerchief.

"You betcha," Scooter agreed, collapsing in his seat, "We might have to ditch these disguises now. They will recognize us following them."

****

Joey whistled a tune inside the cab as they drove through town. The plan had gone off perfectly—perhaps a little too perfectly. Roc and Ks were enjoying themselves too much as well, playing "I spy" as they drove through town. Coming to a traffic light, the light turned red, and they slowed to a stop. Joey tapped his fingers rhythmically on the steering wheel, waiting for the light to change. Suddenly, an ear-piercing BANG interrupted his tapping. The windshield cracked before his very eyes. A bullet had flown through the car! Joey turned around and saw a van racing up behind them. Several men were in the van, brandishing firearms. One took out his AK-47 and discharged half a magazine into the rear of the car, shattering the taillights. Joey revved the engine. The traffic light had not yet changed color.

"Hold on, rocks!" he shouted, and the car squealed out into the intersection.

He veered around the traffic crossing the intersection, causing cars to stop in their tracks. This caused a pile-up, and people began angrily yelling out of their windows. Seeing the intersection blocked, Parker drove the van onto a raised ramp of a flatbed truck. He punched the pedal, and the van soared over the piled-up cars, skimming the roofs of the vehicles. The people suddenly grew quiet after witnessing this feat. The van touched down on all four wheels and continued the chase. Clarkson held his chest, breathing deep.

"Great, driving, Parker!" he said, his face streaked with sweat, "Just don't do it again!"

Roc looked out the back window and saw the van still on their tail.

"Jumping Jehoshaphat! They're still following us!" he exclaimed to Joey.

"Right," Joey noted, "We will just have to shake them!"

He swerved into an alley and drove through the tight backroads. Turning around one building, he stopped the vehicle and looked around. The van was nowhere in sight.

"Did we lose them?" asked Ks, frantically looking around.

"I don't know," Joey replied, looking out the rear window, "I sure hope we did."

Bang! A bullet flew through the front window again! Joey and the rocks turned around and saw the van heading down the alley straight towards them! Joey slammed the transmission into reverse and zipped to the entrance of the alley. The van was approaching rapidly; Joey was only driving in reverse. Joey turned the wheel and did a complete 180, shifting the vehicle back into drive. He put the pedal to the metal and sped back onto the main road. The van followed quickly behind them, and a few men began firing at the cab again. Holes appeared on the back windshield as Joey and the rocks ducked low to avoid the fire. Clarkson took out his handgun and began to shoot at the tires, missing them barely and hitting the low hubcaps that protected the tires.

"If this goes on," exclaimed Roc, "our car will become Swiss cheese!"

"Us too!" screamed Ks.

"I agree," Joey said. He fumbled in his coat with one hand and threw out a derringer and a 9mm handgun. "Use these and aim for their tires but be very sparing with ammo!"

"Oh, sure thing!" grinned Roc. "It's time we return fire!"

Roc took the 9mm and climbed out of the front passenger window halfway. He fired several shots at the van's tires. The shots ricocheted off the van's fender. One hit the rearview mirror, sending it flying past Clarkson's head.

"Curses! They're shooting at us!" Clarkson exclaimed, "Confound them!"

"Holy Swiss!" cried Roc, climbing back in the car, "I missed!"

"What horrible aim you have," said Ks, "You almost hit that guy! Now, let an old gunner show you how it's done."

Ks took the derringer and climbed out of the driver's side rear window. He took aim with the gun and fired a shot, but the bullet just missed one of the front tires. Clarkson wouldn't take it anymore. He snatched an AK-47 from one the thugs and began firing at the cab.

"Hang on!" Joey shouted.

He swerved the car left and right, trying to dodge the fire. Ks was flung back into the cab while Roc lost his balance as well. They both fell into the back seats of the cab and began bouncing up and down like beach balls. Roc grabbed hold of a seatbelt and hung on. Ks grabbed Roc's arm as they tried to keep still. Roc looked at Ks.

"Some gunner you are!" he told him.

"Hey," replied Ks, "it's not easy when you're moving! You have to…"

Bump!

Joey ran over a speed hump. The rocks flew into the roof and tumbled back down to the seats.

"Joey!" they cried, "Be careful!"

"Sorry," Joey apologized, "Doing my best!"

Clarkson climbed back in the van. "We need to be closer!" he shouted to Parker while reloading his gun, "We can't get a solid hit on them!"

"I'm trying," Parker explained, "but it's not easy going fast in this big crate!"

Roc and Ks both peeked out of the rear windows, firing several more shots. Ks's derringer was empty, while Roc's Glock only had a few more shots left. The other two men in the back of the van began to fire as well. The cab wasn't so fancy anymore. Riddled in holes, with the backlights shot out, it was not a pretty sight. Joey turned to the rocks.

"You two drive!" He exclaimed and took the gun from Roc.

Joey and Ks quickly switched places, while Roc jumped down to the floorboard and took control of the pedals. Ks grabbed the wheel and began steering. Joey scrambled into the back seat and hung out of the window, using his arm to stable his gun. Clarkson leaned out of the window to the van. He and Joey were right in line with each other only a few feet away!

"Heh, this'll scare him," Clarkson grinned.

Clarkson turned his firepower towards Joey. The bullets whizzed past Joey's skull, taking his hat off his head. Joey blinked, startled. He switched his aim to Clarkson and fired a shot. The bullet knocked Clarkson's gun right out of his hand! Clarkson looked shocked and began motioning for another gun. Joey took the chance and fired three shots into the tires. The tires fell flat in an instant and the van began to veer and sway. Parker tried his best to keep it from crashing, but they were going just too fast. The van swerved off the road and into a ditch. Joey smiled and climbed back into the cab.

"Great shooting!" cried Ks, taking his eyes off the road.

"Ks!" shouted Joey, pointing straight ahead, "Look out!"

A huge truck was coming straight at them! Ks jumped with all his might on the steering wheel and turned to the left. Roc jumped on the brakes by himself, and the car skidded to another road. To their dismay, the road had a sharp turn with a fence alongside it. Behind the fence were the docks. At the speed they were going, they would punch through the fence and plunge into the sea! Ks pulled left again on the wheel. Roc jumped up and helped him. The car slid right towards the fence! Joey reached over and shoved the wheel left as well. The car turned just in time! The side of the car crashed into the fence. Roc jumped on the brakes and the cab came to a stop. Smoke steamed from the engine. Joey and Ks breathed a sigh of relief. Roc climbed off the floorboard.

"Well!" he said, "That was exhilarating!"

"I don't want another car ride like that again," exclaimed Ks, falling back in the driver seat.

Joey reached into the back seats and pulled out the case. He opened it and examined the statue. He turned it over and examined the bottom of the statue. He could barely make out the X marking, but it could have been worn off due to age. He showed it to the rocks. The rocks smiled at him with gleaming eyes.

"This is the statue!?" Ks almost shrieked.

"It might be!" Joey replied, "Let's get it back to Berlin. We must show the others."

Joey climbed into the driver seat and cranked the engine. The beaten car chugged back to life, and they drove away from the bay, heading back to the train station.

Chapter 10: The Two Strangers

A long, red bus pulled up to a bus stop in Paris. Radford and Scooter jumped to the sound of the horn that interrupted their reading. It was time to start following the statue thieves again.

"I'm getting really tired of trekking all over Europe," Scooter grumbled as he stretched.

"Well, think of it as a vacation," Radford said with a wink.

"I would," replied Scooter, "if we weren't constantly rushing from here to there."

Leaving their seats, they followed the thieves off the bus. The thugs left the bus stop and headed down Avenue des Champs-Élysées, Paris's main street. They abruptly turned into an alley, which Scooter and Radford noticed.

"They might be meeting up with someone down there," Radford whispered to Scooter, "let's listen."

They crept into the alley and hid behind a trashcan. Peering over the trashcan's lid, they watched the men silently. The three men walked up to a back door to one of the buildings. They knocked on the door, and a woman opened it.

"We're here for the suitcase," Stan told her, "Mr. Bernard told us it would be here."

"Just one minute," said the woman in a French accent. She walked back into the building. She came out a few minutes later and handed the men a suitcase.

"The statue is inside," she said, "We pinched it from a collector a few days ago. Make sure not to lose it."

"Don't you worry," replied Stan, as they turned and walked away, "we won't lose it."

Radford and Scooter stood up carefully behind the trash can.

"Come on," whispered Radford, "Let's follow them." They crept away from the trashcan and tiptoed through the alley. All was going well, until *Crunch!* Scooter stepped on an aluminum can! The men spun around and spotted them.

"Hey!" Bill shouted, "They're the punks who attacked us in Berlin!"

The three rolled up their sleeves, they slowly made their way to Radford and Scooter.

"You better keep your distance," Radford exclaimed, "I know karate!"

"Hah!" said Stan, "Yeah right! Boys, get 'em!"

At that moment, two strangers rose out of the shadows and pounced on the thugs. The first one brought down a piece of plywood on Frank. He fell to the ground stunned. Bill turned, and the second stranger shoved a trashcan down on his head and pushed him into a garbage dumpster. Stan spun around and pointed a gun at the two strangers.

"Enough!" he shouted.

Radford took advantage of the moment to karate chopped Stan in the shoulder, instantly dazing him. Stan dropped the gun and fell to the floor. The strangers, two boys in their late teens, picked up the suitcase and handed it to Scooter. One had copper colored hair that almost reached to his shoulders, and the other was blonde, with shaven sides and long bangs over his face.

"Isn't this yours?" one of them asked.

"No," Radford told them, rubbing his sore hand, "But we heard it's been stolen from a local collector."

"Yes," Scooter spoke up, "We believe it might be a valuable cat statue."

The boys looked at each other, and then at Radford and Scooter.

"Do you mean a Ruby Cat?" asked one boy.

"How did you know about that!?" Scooter and Radford asked simultaneously.

"The name's Tommy Lee," said the blonde-haired boy. He pointed to the longhaired boy, "This is my good friend, Ricky. We were always interested in history and traveling the world. We have a YouTube channel called 'The Dudes' Discoveries', in which we travel to different countries to explore their myths and legends."

"We recently learned about the Legend of the Ruby Cat," Ricky added in. "We are still searching, it's ancient history. gonna make a dope video, hopefully getting us tons of views."

He pointed to GoPro's strapped around his and Tommy's chests. "We are filming this right now, so, I hope ya don't mind being in our video," said Ricky. "We'll give a huge shout out to you two."

Radford rubbed his chin, "Hmm, I guess I don't mind if I'm on camera." He turned to Scooter, "You good with that?"

Scooter shrugged. "Sure."

"Ricky and I have to be careful doing this stuff," said Tommy Lee "We've encountered these fellas before, and lemme tell you, it wasn't pleasant."

"You don't tell us," said Scooter, "It seems like Radford, and I bumped into every thug within a five-mile radius."

"We saw you fellas get jumped back in Berlin," Tommy Lee concluded, "The same guys who attacked you two were the same ones we encountered, so we decided to follow you two to make sure you both were okay. Luckily, we were here when you needed us."

"Thank you very much, lads," said Radford, shaking their hands, "My name is Radford Weston, and this is my pal, Scooter Ford. We have another friend with us, and he is on the case as well."

"Really?" said Ricky, "The more dudes the merrier!"

"He's following a thief right now though," Radford answered, "We found a family who lives in Berlin, and they had a Ruby Cat among their possessions. As they were going to give it to us to examine, four men in a black car ambushed them and stole their statue. We tried to help but the thugs overwhelmed us. They sped off in their car. We pursued them following every move they made. That was when we discovered the crooks had split up to throw us off their tracks. Our friend, Joey Packard, chased after the one guy while we followed the trail of these three thugs here."

"So, there's another guy ya'll are chasing," said Ricky, "when we catch up with your friend, we can help you guys sort out this Ruby Cat business."

"No no no," Scooter interrupted, shaking his head, "You two aren't following us. It's too dangerous."

"Aww, come on, bro," Tommy Lee insisted, "We would be a great help to you fellas. Besides, we're already on our own quest ourselves and we helped you two by knocking those thugs out."

"You'll be on our video too!" Ricky added.

"I don't know…" Scooter said slowly.

"It'll be a great idea," Radford exclaimed, "We could use two young strappin' boys to help us. I'm not in fighting shape anyway."

"Aw, heck yeah!" exclaimed the boys, "But we want our share of the cut if we find it." Ricky added.

"That's a done deal," Radford agreed.

Scooter sighed and set the case on a crate nearby. He opened the case very carefully and took out the statue. Radford and the boys came over and looked at it as well. Scooter flipped the statue over and searched the bottom for an X. He looked very closely and saw a faint X etched in the clay. Everyone froze. Tommy Lee yelped in excitement. Radford adjusted his glasses and examined the X marking.

"It looks like a real marking alright," he said, "Nothing phony about it that I can discern."

"Quick," Scooter said as he handed Radford the statue, "I'm going to call Joey. He will be amazed by our find."

Scooter dialed up Joey, paced a few feet away, and began talking excitedly to Joey on the phone about their find. The boys were still eyeing the statue.

"Rubies or no rubies," Radford mused, "I would still like a statue like this one. It would match the banker's lamp I have on my desk."

"Not us, man," said Ricky, "We would each like to get our share and use the money from it to buy a motorcycle. Those would help with our travels in America. Then maybe donate the rest of the moolah."

"Patience, my friends," Radford told them, "We still don't know if the rubies are inside."

"How?" exclaimed Tommy Lee, "It has a freakin' X on it, so it must be real. The only way it couldn't be real is if this whole cat story is fake."

"We will see," Radford reassured them.

"Guys," Scooter shouted to them, "You'll never believe this!"

"What is it?" asked Radford.

"Joey has a cat statue too!" Scooter exclaimed, "And brace yourselves, it has an X on it as well!

"What!?" Radford and the boys shouted, "How is that possible!?"

"I'm not sure," Scooter replied, "This is confusing!"

"Does that mean there are four rubies!?" exclaimed Tommy. "Maybe we could buy two jet skis, also!"

"That can't be possible," Radford told them, "According to the legend, there are only two rubies."

"Who knows?" Ricky said, "The famous legends could get a few details changed over the years."

Scooter walked back to the group. He took the statue from Radford's hands and put in back in the case.

"Joey wants us to meet him in Berlin," he said, closing the case shut, "Obviously; he wants to see the statue for himself."

"Alright," said Radford picking up his case, "Let's go."

****

Joey stepped off the train at the Brussels station, the rocks following close behind. They pushed through the crowded platform and headed to a refreshment stand. Joey bought a bottle of water, sat down on a bench, and had a long drink. The rocks climbed onto the bench and sat beside him. After watching the crowds go by for a few minutes, with a lot of people eyeing the rocks as they passed, Roc spoke up.

"So, how much longer do we have to go?"

"Just a few hours," replied Joey.

"Good!" sighed Roc, leaning back on the bench, "I'll be glad to get this trip over with."

"I agree," said Joey, "It is exhilarating to travel, but after a while it can drain you. That is, unless you are taking a restful vacation, then it's a different story."

Ks suddenly jerked upright. He nudged Joey in the elbow and pointed to the crowd. Four men came marching towards them in a quick manner. They had never seen those men before, which was the suspicious part. Joey quickly got off the bench and grabbed the case. Roc and Ks hopped off the bench with Joey and they briskly walked into the crowd. Joey looked around and saw that the men were still following them.

"Rocks," he whispered, "Get lost in the crowd, hurry. They're still tailing us."

Roc and Ks ran into the thickest part of the crowd and Joey followed suit. They shoved and pushed their way as hard as they could, trying to keep plenty of space between them and the strangers. The men elbowed through the crowd as well, gaining ever so slightly. Joey and the rocks knew they were catching up with them, so they moved faster. People glared at them as they shoved through. All of a sudden, Joey stopped with a jerk. One of the men had grabbed his coat. Joey spun around and gave him a firm, but quick fist to the face. The man fell to the ground, clutching his face. A woman screamed, and a commotion suddenly broke out amongst the throng of people. The strangers could not move on any further. Joey and the rocks ducked behind a concrete retaining wall filled with plants and watched the men disappear in the crowds.

"They're gone," Joey told the rocks.

"Who in the world were they?" asked Ks.

"They obviously weren't friendly," answered Joey, "Probably Clarkson's henchmen."

"I'll bet they have spies watching our every move!" Ks shuddered.

"You're probably right," said Joey, "let's get out of here."

Joey and the rocks slowly rose from behind the plant wall, ran to the ticket booth, and bought three tickets for Berlin. Joey scanned the area, making sure no one was watching them. He and the rocks quickly made their way to the next train's platform.

"I'm going to be honest," said Ks, "I am getting very tired of train travel."

"Same," Roc added, "I don't even want to see or hear another train for a long time."

"Stop grumbling, Rocks," Joey scolded them, "We need to leave this place now! Those thugs aren't going to let us get away that easily!"

They sprinted onto the train and Joey gave the tickets to the conductor. They hastily found their seats and sat down with a huff. Finally, they were on their way to Berlin.

"I really think this is the last train ride we will be taking," Joey told the rocks.

"I hope so," said Roc, "or I might just go crazy!"

The train blew its whistle and began to pull out of the station. As it pulled out, Joey looked through the window, watching the station glide by, like a slide presentation. He turned his head and saw, standing on the platform, the same men who had been chasing them! Their eyes locked as they spotted Joey in the train's window while the train rolled away. Joey relaxed in his seat and breathed a sigh of relief. He was glad they were leaving those hooligans behind!

Chapter 11: More than One Ruby Cat

Splash! A red bus drove through a muddy puddle. It chugged over the hills and through the valleys; Scooter and Radford were among its passengers. They still couldn't believe what they were holding. Another Ruby Cat with the same X marking as the original statue? It was phenomenal! They would be glad to meet Joey again and show him this amazing find. Tommy Lee and Ricky still stared at the statue as the bus drove along through the countryside. They jerked out of their stare as the bus came to a stop at the next station…Berlin.

"We're here," said Radford, "Joey will be amazed at what we found."

"Wouldn't surprise me," Scooter added, "It sure caught us off-guard."

"Where are we meeting him?" asked Ricky.

"Berlin Town Square," Scooter replied, "He told us to wait there."

Nearby, a street vendor was handing coffee to a customer. The customer had deep-set eyes with a scar down his left cheek. His bushy, brown eyebrows sat straight on his brow, almost touching across. With all the strange tattoos running up and down his arms, one would easily assume he was associated with a gang. He turned his head and saw the four comrades step off the bus. He grabbed his coffee to take a long drink, and then slammed the cup down on the counter, the coffee splashed on the counter. The vendor grumbled under his breath and began wiping up the mess.

The unsavory customer then took his phone out of his coat and dialed up a number.

"Hey, boss? It's me, Ardanan."

"Ah, what do you got for me, my friend?"

"The four birds have walked in the trap."

"Excellent. You know what to do."

"Of course, time to slam the cage shut. What about you, sir, you at the rendezvous?"

"I'm currently at Big Statue in Berlin, if you know what I mean."

"I understand completely, sir."

The man put the phone in his pocket and quickly walked away from the counter. He motioned to a gang of thugs lurking nearby, who started to follow him. Stalking Radford, Scooter, and the boys as they walked down the street. They had their clubs and guns in coats at the ready.

"Alright, we're gonna take them out, one by one," Ardanan told his men, "First, grab the old man, and then take care of that spikcy haired kid. The other two boys should be easy to handle after that."

The men nodded and they all got in position. Two of them, Herbert and Parker, quickly strode ahead on the opposite side of street and sat on a bench in front of them. The other two, Ardanan himself and Norman, crept up from behind and started walking casually to avoid suspicion. Ardanan gave them the nod, and the men sprang into action. Norman ran up behind Radford and seized him by the arm. Scooter and the boys jumped back in surprise.

"Radford!" exclaimed Scooter, and he tried to free Radford from Norman. However, a quick fist to the face from Norman immediately quelled his action. Scooter went sprawling to the ground, and the Ardanan grabbed him with an iron grip. Tommy Lee and Ricky ran to aid their friends and shoved Ardanan off Scooter. Ricky then charged Ardanan throwing punches, ready to strike. Ardanan easily dodged the blows and stuck his leg in front of Ricky, causing him to trip. Tommy Lee lifted his leg to kick Ardanan, but the man quickly thumped Tommy Lee with his fist. Tommy Lee fell to the ground. Parker and Herbert, stationed down the street, joined the struggle and grabbed the boys, holding them tight. A van pulled up to the curb and stopped. Ardanan took out his phone and dialed the boss.

"Sir, we caught the birds."

"Excellent! Bring them to the Big Statue immediately."

"You got it, sir."

Ardanan glared at Radford, Scooter, and the boys. "You're coming with us," he barked at them, "The boss wants to talk to you at the Big Cat."

"And what exactly is the *Big Cat*?" Radford asked with an eyebrow raised.

"You'll soon see," smirked Ardanan, turning and walking towards the van. The men led the four prisoners at gunpoint into the rear of the van and locked the doors. Ardanan climbed into the passenger seat.

"Let's move," he told the driver.

The driver nodded. He put the gear into drive, and they drove off to their mysterious destination.

****

A taxicab pulled up to the Berlin Train Station. The driver beeped his horn and began drumming with his fingers. He looked towards the station. Ah, his passengers had arrived. Joey and the rocks climbed into the back seats.

"Where to, sir?" asked the driver.

"Berlin Town Square," Joey answered, buckling his seatbelt, "I have a few friends to meet up with there."

"Alrighty then,"

The driver beeped his horn again to warn the other vehicles passing nearby. He pulled out of the station and drove towards Town Square. After arriving at their destination, Joey paid the fare and he and the rocks climbed out of the cab. They walked to the meeting spot they had agreed upon and sat on a bench. Joey and the rocks gawked at the amazing old buildings surrounding the town's square. The hustle and bustle of people going to and from their destinations was hypnotic to watch. A few minutes went by, then fifteen, then thirty. Joey began to wonder what was stalling Radford and Scooter.

"Well, where are they?" asked Roc, suddenly.

"Perhaps their train was delayed?" wondered Joey.

Joey pulled out his phone and dialed Radford. After a few seconds of ringing, Radford still didn't pick up.

"Spigots," Joey grumbled, "They won't pick up either."

"Ha!" Roc laughed, "They are probably sleeping on the train."

"What do we do while we wait?" Ks said, looking around Town Square.

"Let's rent some sort of transportation, then we could look around the city. Afterwards, we could head back to the ceramic shop and give that family their statue back."

"Sounds good," Ks agreed.

Joey picked up the suitcase and they began their tour of Town Square. In his mind, he really hoped Radford and Scooter were only delayed by a late train, and not in real trouble.

****

Mr. Bernard tapped his fingers on his chair. He stroked his chin and looked at his watch. It was almost time for the "guests" to arrive. Clarkson sat nearby on a waiting bench near the front desk of the ceramic shop. Beside him, Stan, Bill, and Frank leaned against the wall, snoozing. Mr. Bernard lifted his head when he heard a car pull up to the ceramic shop. He looked out the shop's window and nodded. They were here. He walked to the back room of the shop and called to the boss.

"Mr. Gregory," he said, "They're here."

Mr. Gregory Woods smiled and put down his wine glass. He was a stout man suited with a tight green jacket. A gold chain attached to a pocket watch was stuffed halfway in his jacket pocket. He had long sideburns running down his face, connected to his beard. His hair was brown, but the grey could be seen peeking through his temples. The man had an aura of seniority, but also the presence of leadership about him. His men respected him and his class, doing his every deed without little to no resistance or arguments. They knew he would pay them for their work, and the man paid well.

He slowly got out of his seat and walked past Mr. Bernard to the front of the shop. He ordered his butler to open the front door. The butler opened the door, and Ardanan and his men bustled in with Radford, Scooter, and the boys in tow. Mr. Gregory smiled in satisfaction. He was victorious. The troublemakers were now under his control; nothing stood in his way. He picked up another glass of his finest red wine and took a sip. He smacked his lips and eyed the prisoners.

"So, you're the bothersome busybodies," he smirked, "trying to steal my treasure!"

"We aren't stealing your treasure," Radford retorted, "You stole the Abel family's treasure!"

"You mean this family?" asked Mr. Gregory, with smug sarcasm, waving a hand to the door of the back room.

Out of the room came Bert and Alice, followed by their parents and grandparents. Behind them were two of Gregory's ruffians, pushing them along. The family saw

Radford and Scooter and glared at them. Suddenly, Mrs. Maria ran up to Radford and grabbed his coat.

"You said the curse wouldn't harm us!" she yelled in his face, "Now our family is in peril because of you!"

One guard pulled her back to the family. She buried her face in her apron and wept. Mr. Klaus wrapped his arm around her shoulder.

Mr. Gregory sighed, annoyed. "Ardanan, hand me the suitcase," he said, pointing to the briefcase.

Ardanan took the case from Norman and handed it to Mr. Gregory.

"You see," he said, "Your friend took the wrong statue when he snuck into our mansion. We put our statues in identical cases. Your friend took another statue we found in Brussels a few weeks ago. He thinks he has your statute, Mr. Klaus, but he does not. Clarkson opened the suitcase your friend left behind after he got away with the other statue. He found out the cases had been misplaced. Your pal has the one we found at Brussels; and if it has the rubies or not, we don't know. Your statue and the one from Brussels both have X's on them, making it all very confusing. Con artists around the world must be etching fake X's on these cat statues to gain profit from statues of no value," he pointed to Radford, Scooter and the boys,

"That might be the reason why the one your friends seized from our hideout in Paris also has an X on it."

Mr. Gregory set the two brief cases on the table. He opened the suitcase that Radford and his friends had found, and the statue out carefully. He scrutinized the bottom of the statue.

"As you can see," he explained, "Here's the X. Now comes the difficult part. The only way we can find out if it is the real one is to break it open and free the rubies from their casket. It's going to be a pity to break this beautiful work of art, but how will we know what's inside? You got to break a few eggs to make an omelet."

Mr. Gregory sighed and rubbed his hand over the fine artisanship. Without warning, he lifted the statue over his head and hurdled it to the floor. Pieces of the statue flew everywhere, but there were no rubies amongst the scattered rubble. Mr. Gregory raised an eyebrow.

"Well, this isn't the real one," he turned to the other suitcase, "Process of elimination, that's how* we will find out which one is real."

Mr. Gregory carefully removed the cat statue from the second case. He looked at the bottom of the statue and showed the X to everyone present.

"Look, another X. We believe this is the genuine one," he said, "No real evidence…but just a gut feeling."

"You can't destroy that statue!" Mr. Klaus exclaimed, "It's been in our family for generations!"

"Please, sir," Alice begged, "that's one of our heirlooms! Don't break it, please don't!"

"Sorry, child," Mr. Gregory sighed, "Tradition was made to be broken."

Mr. Gregory stepped in front of everyone in the room and lifted the statue above his head once again. With a mighty heave, he threw the statue to the ground. Shards of porcelain flew all over the floor. The family gasped to see their most prized possession was destroyed. Mr. Gregory breathed in deep to hold back a burst of anger. The statue contained no rubies. Ardanan and his men, Parker, Herbert, and Norman, sifted through the fragments on the floor, but to no avail.

"Well," Mr. Gregory grumbled in disappointment, "Your statue doesn't seem to have the rubies. What a misfortunate thing to happen. Two fakes but no rubies. That means your friend might have the real one, the one from Brussels."

Bert clinched his fists and looked at Mr. Gregory. With a burst of speed, he ran into him, knocking Gregory to the floor.

"You monster!" cried Bert, clenching his fists.

Two men nearby pulled him away from Gregory and shoved him back near his parents. Mr. Gregory got up from the floor and gave a sharp look to Bert.

"Little brat," he muttered.

"Leave the kid alone," exclaimed Ricky, "You jerks just destroyed their family treasure!"

Mr. Gregory scoffed at Ricky and motioned for Clarkson to come near to him.

"Get them into the van," he whispered, "We're taking these folks with us."

"We are?" asked Clarkson, "won't that be a lot of trouble?"

"We have no choice," Mr. Gregory replied, "If we don't, they will go to the police in a heartbeat and then we'd end up in jail."

"You're right, sir," said Clarkson, motioning to his men. The men nodded and began rounding up the prisoners. Just then, the sound of a motorbike could be heard outside the door. A knock followed it soon after.

"Hey guys," a voice said on the other side of the door, "We're back!"

Ardanan opened the door and gasped. He couldn't believe who stood there.

"I've got the statue!" Joey exclaimed, unaware of who it was, "And it…has…an…X!"

Quick as a flash, Ardanan ripped the case out of Joey's hand. Joey was speechless. Mr. Bernard and Clarkson were right in front of him face to face. The same men he tricked as a cab driver now had his friends in custody.

"GET HIM!" Mr. Gregory shouted.

"Spigots!" cried the rocks.

Clarkson ran forward, but Joey slammed the door in his face. Clarkson fell to the ground, stunned.

"Bernard, help Clarkson get rid of these freaks!" ordered Mr. Gregory, pulling out a handgun, "Ardanan, take the prisoners and follow me!"

Ardanan, Herbert, Norman, and Parker drug the prisoners out the back door, along with Mr. Gregory. Clarkson's men closed in on Joey and the rocks, taking out their mini clubs. Mr. Bernard took out his gun.

"Alright, rocks," Joey told them, "Time to fight!"

Stan charged at Joey and swung his club at him. Joey dove below the club and shoved Stan in the stomach with his shoulder. He pushed Stan through the doorway into Frank, which sent them both into a shelf filled with ceramic pots. Out of the corner of his eye, Joey saw Bill raise his club. He dodged the swing and jammed his elbow into Bill's hand. Bill howled and dropped the club. Mr. Bernard couldn't get a good shot with all the fighting going on. Joey snatched up the club and threw it at Mr. Bernard, striking him square in the face. Mr. Bernard dropped his gun and stumbled towards the door, attempting to escape.

"I got this!" Ks exclaimed.

Ks jumped in front of Mr. Bernard and got under his heel. They both rolled out the door. Ks and Bernard lay in the street on their backs.

"Two points!" said Ks, dizzy.

Joey took off his coat and threw it around Bill. He spun Bill around and threw him into the front desk, but Bill managed to regain his senses. Bill and Joey circled the desk like boxers, ready to strike. As Bill lunged forward Joey, quick as a striking snake, caught his head and slammed his face on the desk. Bill slid to the floor, this finally knocked Bill out cold. Frank, the last one standing, came up behind Joey and raised his club. Roc burst out of the window curtains and jumped on Frank, wrapping his head in the curtains. Roc's weight threw Frank off balance, and the thug collapsed to the ground with a thud.

Nearby, Clarkson moaned, and slowly began to regain consciousness. Joey spotted him attempting to get up, and he struck him with his fist. Clarkson sprawled onto the floor, out for good this time.

Joey stepped over Clarkson and ran out the back door. The van was just starting to take off. Obviously, Radford and Scooter had put up a fight to give him some time. Joey pulled a police tracker out of his pocket and threw it at the van. The tracker flew through the air and stuck to the van's back doors. Joey ran back into the shop, picking up his coat.

"Rocks!" he called, putting his coat on, "Hurry! We need to chase that van!"

Roc and Ks hopped over the unconscious thugs and followed Joey. They scampered out the back door and ran to their motor nearby. Joey jumped on the bike and cranked the engine. The engine rumbled to life. Roc and Ks hopped into the sidecar. Joey took out his SD and handed it to the rocks. The tracking device beeped red on the map of Berlin. Joey revved the engine and sped off in the direction the van took.

****

Mr. Gregory leaned back in his seat. The Ruby Cat was now his! Things could only get better from here. Just then, his ear caught the sound of a motorcycle approaching rapidly from behind their van. He looked in the rear-view mirror to see Joey and the rocks following them.

"That blasted fool is on our tail again," he scoffed to Ardanan, "Try to lose him!"

"Got it, boss," Ardanan said as he swerved around a corner, trying to lose Joey in the traffic.

Joey kept an eye on the van as a hawk would a mouse. The streets of Berlin were tight, and it was risky driving at such high speeds. He saw Herbert and Norman open the back doors of the van. Joey saw everyone crammed in the tied behind their backs. One of the men grabbed an empty wooden crate and pushed it out of the van. The crate fell on the road and shattered into a dozen pieces.

"Hold on, rocks!" Joey shouted.

He revved the engine and swerved hard to avoid the flying debris. The wooden pieces flew by, missing the bike by inches. Ardanan's men growled and took out their handguns. They shot at Joey, no doubt with intent to kill. Joey ducked below the motorbike's windshield as the bullets whizzed overhead. Roc pulled out a derringer out of Joey's coat.

"Spigots, Roc!" Joey exclaimed, "Don't shoot! You might hit our friends!"

"Oh, you're right," Roc said as he put the gun down.

In the van, Scooter was sitting closet to the men were shooting at Joey. He moved himself along the back of the van to the thugs and gave Norman a mighty kick, which nearly pushed him out of the van. Herbert grabbed his shirt and yanked him back inside. They were furious and gave Scooter a smack across the face. Joey took the opportunity to pull around to the driver's side of the van.

"Ks," he exclaimed, "Take my mirror out of my pocket and shine it in the driver's eyes!"

"Got it!" yelled Ks. He fumbled through Joey's coat and pulled out the mini mirror. He angled it to the right position that would directly shine the sun into Adranan's eyes. Ardanan blinked and held a hand in front of his eyes, but it was difficult for him to drive with one hand at such high speed. He gripped both hands on the wheel and swerved towards Joey, trying to ram Joey's motorbike. Joey braked sharply, narrowly missing being smashed by the van. The jerking of the brakes caused Ks to drop the mirror, which shattered into a thousand pieces on the street.

"Ooh," the rocks shivered, "Seven years of bad luck."

"You two seriously think our luck can get any worse?" Joey exclaimed, "Hold on! We are going to try again!"

Joey revved the bike to catch up to the van once more. They entered the crowded part of town now, and even traveling at a slower speed, navigating through the tight streets was tough. Ardanan blasted the horn on the van, as people scrambled out of the way and cars swerved out of the way. Joey followed close behind, dodging innocent bystanders and vehicles that were in the streets. The van skimmed parked cars as it thundered down the streets. Mr. Gregory was getting tired of this game and gave Parker his gun. Parker smirked and squeezed out several shots at Joey. All the shots hit the bike, causing it to smoke.

"That's not good!" Joey shouted. He looked ahead and had an idea, "Rocks! We are coming up to a pile of gravel beside the road! Grab a few chunks of it and take out that guy's gun!"

Joey drove the bike near the pile of rocks and Roc and Ks swiped up a few pieces of gravel as they sped by. He pulled behind the van and swerved to the left and right so Parker wouldn't be able to get a good shot at him.

"Get them now rocks!" he exclaimed.

Roc and Ks threw the gravel pieces at Parker's hand. One large chunk landed a hit on Parker's knuckles. Parker yelped and dropped the gun. Joey pulled up right behind the van and Roc and Ks jumped inside. They pounded down Parker and Herbert with one jump. Norman picked up a pipe and swung at the rocks. Roc and Ks jumped clear of the pipe, but dodging it wasn't easy due to the swerving of the van. Roc jumped on top of Norman while Ks ran to the prisoners.

"You all jump outta this van while Roc distracts the crooks!" he exclaimed.

He yanked the ropes off Ricky and Tommy Lee's hands. Tommy Lee spotted an upcoming patch of sand, and they jumped out of the van into the mound. Ks untied Radford and Scooter's ropes next. Scooter didn't wait for any sand; he jumped out of the van and landed with a roll on the road. Joey swerved sharply to avoid his tumbling friend.

"Your turn," Ks told Radford and the family.

"Ks," Radford said somberly, "We cannot jump."

"Huh?" Ks asked, confused, "Why not? We need to get you guys out of this van!"

"We can't," Radford sighed, "There is no way I and the grandparents can survive that jump, let alone the kids. You need to think of another plan when the vehicle stops, wherever that it is."

"But…" Ks was about to say more, when Norman swung at him with the pipe. Ks jumped out of the way as the pipe hit the van's floor with a clang.

"I'm going to finish you two, here and now!" Norman bellowed.

Roc and Ks looked to Radford, who gave them the nod to leave. Reluctantly, the two jumped out of the van just before Norman could hit them again with the pipe. They tumbled and rolled on the road as Joey and the van drove out of sight.

Still in pursuit, Joey swerved around to the driver's side of the van once again and pulled his gun out of his pocket. He pointed it at Ardanan through the van's window.

"Pull this vehicle over NOW!"

"Not on your life!" shouted Ardanan and drove the van into Joey's bike.

The van smashed the sidecar. Joey swayed on the bike but managed to keep it straight. Ardanan cursed in frustration. He looked up ahead in the street and saw an opportunity. He drove alongside Joey and shoved him almost onto the sidewalk. The smell of burnt rubber filled the air. Joey held his position and viewed the road ahead. Construction equipment occupied the lane ahead, totally blocking the road! Joey tried to avoid the lane, but pedestrians crowded the sidewalk to his left. The van was on his right. He clenched the brakes with all the force he could muster, but it wasn't enough! The bike smashed into the construction equipment. Joey flew over the handlebars and into the construction site. The bike tumbled repeatedly until it burst into flames. Gregory and Ardanan snorted in laughter as they looked in the rear-view mirror. The bike lay in the road flickering with flames and billowing smoke. The rider was nowhere to be seen...

Chapter 12: Rethinking Plans

A young man in a dusty trench coat walked up to a coffee shop. The bell rang as he entered; people turned their attention to the rough-looking figure. He ordered a coffee at the counter and headed back outside to sit at the tables. The waitress hurried with the order a bit quicker than usual. She picked up his coffee and walked outside to her customer. She nearly dropped the cup in surprise. Two rocks were standing next to the customer. The waitress managed to keep her composure and set down the coffee cup.

"Here's your coffee, sir," she said professionally, despite still being startled by sentient rocks.

"Thank you." Joey replied. He picked up the cup and took a long drink. Joey leaned back in the chair, watching the scenery. The coffee shop was the "Father Carpenter," a shop surrounded by buildings. It had a few tables and chairs in the front of the building, as well as a nice square with over a dozen tables in its center. A fountain and a row of bushes decorated the square. It was a peaceful little spot to sit and contemplate. For a few minutes, not a word was spoken. Roc decided to break the silence.

So…what's our plan?"

"Don't have any," Joey said abruptly, putting down the mug. "I've used up my thinking capacity. They could be long gone; in another country even."

"We're done then?" said Ks.

"I never said that," Joey answered, "I just need some time to rethink everything."

"What about using the tracker we threw on the van?" Roc asked.

"It's not showing on the scanner anymore," Joey sighed, "Apparently they discovered and smashed it."

Suddenly, along came Scooter and the two boys trudging up the small walk path to the cafe. Scooter saw Joey and ran up to him.

"Joey!" he exclaimed, "Say, are you hurt? You look like ya got flung off a horse!"

"It was a bike," Joey replied, "But I'm fine now."

"Oh," said Scooter. He then waved his hand to the boys, "Well, I have a few new friends here, Ricky and Tommy Lee. They helped us get back the Ruby Cat after a few crooks stole it. Well, the fake one that is…"

Joey lit up, "You were the two chaps I saw at the Berlin library. You were reading that book on the Ruby Cat."

"Yeah," Tommy Lee nodded, "and you were that guy spying on us. We were looking into the Ruby Cat mystery because we thought it would make a sick video for our YouTube channel."

"We first saw the statue at New Orleans Central Square," added Ricky.

"That's exactly where I found out about the Ruby Cat," Joey said in awe, "It's amazing how we both learned of the legend at the same place and time."

Suddenly Tommy Lee let out a scream, and took a step back, "What in the pits of shell are those!?"

Ricky stared, "Bro, they look creepy as heck!"

"What? Who?" Ks asked.

"You!" the two boys shouted.

Ks turned to Roc, "Do I have dirt on my face or something?"

Roc squinted, "Uh, no, I don't think so…"

"Oh, sorry about that," Scooter apologized, "We forgot to tell you about Roc and Ks. They are talking *and* walking rocks, as absurd as that sounds."

"How in the world is that even possible!?" Tommy Lee exclaimed.

"It's a long story," Joey answered, "I myself don't even know everything. But according to them, they've been around for a long time."

"Ahem," Roc interrupted, "Ks and I are here, and we both hear you."

Tommy Lee and Ricky were still shaking, but after a few minutes, they managed to calm down.

"Well, as long as they don't bite," said Tommy Lee taking a deep breath, "They're cool with me."

"And with me," Ricky agreed as he sat in a chair, still eyeing the rocks. He forgot about his fear as soon as his mind turned back to the Ruby Cat, "I still can't believe we lost that statue, we had it in our hands."

"Actually, we didn't," Scooter corrected, "Joey did though, but the Ruby Cat we had was a fake. There were no rubies inside. Same goes for the Abels' Ruby Cat, the one Mr. Gregory threw to the ground."

"Yeah, there's something about Mr. Gregory," Joey said, staring into space, "I thought I've seen his face somewhere, but I can't quite single it out."

"I'm wondering why they drew the X on the other Ruby Cat," Tommy Lee pondered.

"Same here," agreed Ricky.

"The answer is to that is obvious, they must have wanted to trick a customer into buying a fake," Roc explained, "That way, they would get a high price for a statue of no value."

"It fooled us for sure," said Scooter, "We thought it was the genuine thing. I can see why it would fool someone else."

Ricky slouched back in his chair, "Ugh! This is embarrassing! We gave it one hundred percent, and still got kicked under the rug."

"I believe it's time for us to give up and accept the facts," Tommy solemnly said, "No use fighting back against something we can't handle."

"Hey now, let's not get down in the dumps," Scooter reassured them, "We'll think of somethin'."

"You're right, I guess," Tommy said quietly, "But still…"

Joey sat up straight in his chair, interrupting Tommy Lee, "Wait, wait…I just remembered!"

He turned to the rocks, "Rocks, do you remember that old mansion we went to?"

"Yeah," Ks answered, "What about it?"

"As I was walking through the living room, I found a picture of a funeral. I'm guessing the owner of the house died."

"Yes, yes," Roc prompted, "Go on."

"Anyways, in the picture there was a teenage boy in the photo attending a funeral. I now know why he looked so familiar; he was Mr. Gregory!"

"How did you know it's Mr. Gregory when that was a teenage kid?" Roc asked, "Mr. Gregory is now way into his late 40s."

"Anatomy," Joey explained, "The human body, once it reaches a certain age, stops growing. For the most part, someone in their late teens will have the same features until they reach adulthood. The nose, the jaw line, brow, shoulders, those all stay pretty much the same. I recognized Mr. Gregory's facial features from seeing the picture of him in that mansion."

"Huh," Ks said, "So Mr. Gregory is part of the Woods family, he has ties to that old mansion we, uh, *visited*."

"You also said you found cat statues in the mansion as well," Roc added, "similar to the ones we found here."

"So, coming here to Berlin," Joey concluded, "Mr. Gregory found the statue, or at least he thinks he did, and now he's taking it back to New Orleans! That explains all the cat statues there. He's been looking for the real Ruby Cat one by one for months, heck, probably years."

"That's great and all," Ricky added, "But how will we catch up to them? They are probably on their way to New Orleans now."

"I know how to handle that," Joey told him, "Radford and I have a friend in London who's a piolet, his name is Mr. Shudman I'll ask if he could lend us one of his planes."

"Awesome!" the two boys said in unison. "Let's go!"

"Wait," Joey halted them, "We need a real plan this time. There's no use charging them and getting caught again. We need to be strategic in our planning."

"Right," Ks said, "We know they are going to the mansion, or at least, that's what we think. So, we need to catch them inside the house. We should build a war mech. Yeah! That would work!"

"Uh, Ks," Roc pointed out, "Those aren't real."

"Yeah, they are!" Ks said, "War mechs are real, alright,"

"Even if they were real, we couldn't afford it." Roc added.

"Afford it, ha! We could build one!"

"Couldn't,"

"Could too,"

"All right, rocks," Scooter interrupted, "Let's turn it back a few steps."

"Wait," Joey exclaimed, "I have an idea!"

"What is it?" Scooter and the rocks asked.

"I'll tell you soon," Joey said, "but first let's go to Mr. Shudman's airstrip. We can discuss the plan on the ride back to New Orleans."

Joey quickly handed a tip to the waitress and thanked her. He dug in his pocket and pulled out his phone. He pulled up a map of England to locate Shudman's Airport.

"It will take us about an hour to get to London by plane from Berlin," said Joey, "We will need to spend the night here though before we leave. It's getting very late. Mr. Gregory may be in New Orleans before us, but we need the rest. We are leaving first thing tomorrow."

They high tailed it to a nearby hotel to rest for the night; they were going to need all their energy for the next day.

****

Mr. Gregory and his gang arrived at the London dock and got ready for the sail back to America. Mr. Gregory's own private cargo ship was waiting to take them across the ocean. The men rounded up Radford and the family, escorted them onto the boat, and took them to the living quarters of the ship. They showed them their place to stay.

"This is where you will stay," Mr. Gregory said smiling, "Hope you enjoy the trip."

"And what are you going to do with us?" Radford asked.

"I can't let you go; you'll call the police. I guess I gotta keep you locked up for the time being," Mr. Gregory answered.

"You can't do that!" Mr. Klaus shouted.

"I will do what I think is best for my business," Mr. Gregory snapped. He turned to Ardanan, "Lock 'em up."

Ardanan shoved the family and Radford into their room and locked the cabin door. He followed Mr. Gregory to the captain's room. Mr. Gregory sat at the head of the captain's table and pulled out a map from a drawer under the table. The captain of the ship and Ardanan pulled up two chairs to the table and sat down. Mr. Gregory spread the map across the table. He ran his finger across the map and stopped at New Orleans.

"There," he said pointing at the location, "That's where my mansion is. The mansion was supposed to be my sister-in-law's after Mr. Woods, my brother, died, but I pulled the strings in my favor. So, my sister-in-law ended up giving me ownership of the mansion, thinking I would help her fix it up."

"So, did you?" asked the captain.

"No…not yet at least," Mr. Gregory rolled up the map, "I'm planning to turn the mansion into a museum. The Ruby Cat is the last piece in my exhibit for the museum. Now that I am certain I have the real Ruby Cat, my journey is coming to an end."

"A museum," Ardanan repeated, "You went through all this trouble just to put the rubies in some dusty ol' museum? Why not sell them and get rich quick? Museums in themselves aren't even that profitable."

"I am a man of history, Ardanan," Gregory replied, "I find joy in collecting artifacts showing them off to the public. You must play the long run game. Having the rubies in my museum will attract a lot of visitors. More importantly, it will draw in educated people–scientists, historians, and scholars. The wealthy men and women who invest in those fields will want to partnership with me. That's what will generate the big bucks, the fame, and influence in New Orleans. I will have a longer lasting impact on the world than just selling them and poof! I disappear into time. And I will do anything to get that fame and recognition I rightfully deserve."

The room grew quiet for a moment after Gregory had finished his speech. The dull hum of the ship's engine resonated throughout the room.

"So, where are your relatives now?" the captain asked, breaking the silence.

"They are living in an apartment now," Mr. Gregory chuckled, "Don't worry; they will be fine."

The captain got back to work navigating the boat, and Ardanan left the office. Mr. Gregory sighed to himself in the chair. He did feel a little sorry for his relatives, but he had had this scheme planned out for a long time now. It was time to put the weak things, like familial affection, behind him. He rose out of the chair and looked out the window. The sun was setting over the waters, turning the sea to a bright orange. The ship's horn blasted as the ship left the harbor and traveled out across the calm sea.

****

Joey threw the last of the luggage into the plane's trunk. He headed to the passenger compartment where the rest of the group was waiting. The plane was a private, two-engine, Bombardier Global 5000, silver in color. It had fifteen seats arranged in two, tight rows.

It was nearly a full 24 hours since the group had last seen Mr. Gregory, but they were finally on their way. Mr. Shudman walked up to the plane and watched as the four climbed aboard.

"Thanks for letting us use one of your planes, Mr. Shudman," Joey said shaking his hand.

"No problem, mate," Mr. Shudman replied, "Just take care of 'er and my pilot."

"We will sir," Joey reassured him.

Joey climbed aboard the plane and shut the swing door, waving to Mr. Shudman. The pilot of the plane flipped the control levers, and the plane's engines roared to life. The plane started to move slowly down the runway. After gaining sufficient speed, the plane lifted slowly into the air. It wasn't long before Mr. Shudman's airport looked like a scale model by the sea.

"So!" Roc asked, "What's your plan?"

"Alright," Joey replied, turning around to face the group, "Gather around and listen closely."

Chapter 13: The Woods

Radford sat in a wooden chair near the window of the ship, quietly thinking to himself. It had been at least two days since the start of their voyage as prisoners. The Abels sat on the bunk, huddled together. Mr. Klaus took a deep breath and sat straight up.

"Well, will your friends be able to find us?" he asked Radford. "Or will they just give up and quit all together?"

"I'm sure they won't give up," Radford told him, "Just because they failed once won't shake them into quitting."

"Mr. Weston," Mrs. Maria somberly spoke up, "I appreciate your kindness to our family. I regret the way I acted towards you a few days ago. Can you forgive my behavior?"

"No hard feelings, ma'am," Radford smiled, "I forgive you. Now's not the time for us to be holding petty grudges."

"Mr. Weston," Mr. Klaus spoke up, "What keeps you optimistic? Here we are locked away in a ship, and yet you still aren't angry or discouraged."

"Oh, trust me, my good man," Radford answered, "I am very capable of breaking down or throwing a fit at any moment. The thing is I know it won't help us at all. I also have hope knowing our friends won't give up on finding us."

"But how do you keep your hope in a time like this? What gives you hope?"

Radford thought for a moment about how to answer the question. A glimmer of light caught his eye; it was the sun reflecting off Mr. Klaus's watch. He asked if he could look at it and the father agreed. Radford held the watch up for everyone to see.

"I might have an answer for you sir," he explained, "Look at this watch. All the little gears inside this simple but complex machine work together to make time "tick", you could say. Now, did this watch just come from nowhere?"

"No," Mr. Klaus chuckled, "A skilled watchmaker had to make all the parts work together."

"Exactly," Radford beamed, "This world, this universe, is the same way. It "tics" and so does everything in it, just like a watch. It was created by the great Watchmaker. Now, the Watchmaker of this earth treasured His creation so much that He couldn't stand to let the dirt and grime get into in His watch. So, He made a special cleaning solution to clean the dirt and grime off His watch. We are the watches. He looks after us and cleans us, if we allow Him. That gives me hope to keep plugging away when life gets rough. I am still afraid many times, but knowing the Watchmaker will look over his watch, I have hope that I will see the next day."

"But don't you believe in curses," Mrs. Maria spoke up, "Curses are no joke, and have many powers with them."

"Oh, believe me, I do believe that curses can and do exist, and they aren't anything to play with," Radford replied, "but I have hope knowing there's a greater Power than any curse…"

The ship's horn blasted loudly and interrupted them. Radford looked out the window and saw a familiar land, the Port of New Orleans. Their journey had come full circle. The clanking of the door lock brought him to attention. The steel door opened and Ardanan, Parker, Norman, and Herbert entered.

"Everyone up," Ardanan said, banging on the door, "We've arrived."

Radford let out a long sigh and rose out of his chair and walked out the door. The Abels followed behind, being escorted by Norman, Herbert, and Parker. Ardanan led the way off the ship. Mr. Gregory was on the dock, waiting, as Ardanan walked up to him.

"The prisoners are ready, sir," he informed him.

"Good," Mr. Gregory replied, "If anyone asks, these people are my guests. Get them in the truck and take them to the mansion. I will be there in a few hours."

"Yes sir," said Ardanan, "but where are you going?"

"I'm going to visit my relatives and tell them what's going on," Mr. Gregory answered.

"Do we want them to know about this?" Ardanan asked again.

"Don't worry. I'm not telling them anything confidential; I'm just going to inform them about the state of the house."

Ardanan nodded and escorted the prisoners to the large truck. Mr. Gregory walked over to his personal cab and climbed in. He tapped the sleeping driver on the shoulder and woke him up.

"Take me to the bank, please. And then take me to the Sonder at the Vitascope, where my relatives live," he said, leaning back in his seat.

"Right away, sir," the driver said, yawning. He cranked the keys and slowly pulled out of the docks.

Mr. Gregory sighed and looked out the window. Now came the hardest part of it all, meeting his relatives. He breathed in deeply and thought of the right words to say.

****

A plane circled over the Port of New Orleans. Joey looked down and pointed out the window.

"There's Mr. Gregory's ship!" he exclaimed.

"I don't see anyone getting in or out of the ship," Roc said, "They could be long gone already."

"It's time we put our plan into action," Joey said.

The pilot circled the harbor until it was the correct height to land on the runway at the New Orleans Lakefront Airport. The jet rolled several hundred meters before it came to a stop. After a few minutes of flipping switches, the pilot shut off the engines.

Joey, Scooter, and the boys picked up their bags. Joey opened the plane's door and stepped out onto the runway, breathing in deep; the smell of Lake Pontchartrain refreshed him after a long flight. Scooter and the others followed suit. Joey waved thanks to the pilot, and the pilot waved back.

"It's great to be back where we belong!" Ks exclaimed, "In good ol' New Orleans!"

"Hurry!" Joey said, flagging down the nearest cab, "We got to get on their trail before it grows cold."

After a half an hour cab ride, they entered the wharf. Joey scanned the crowds for any signs of Mr. Gregory or his men. To his disappointment, there was none.

"Stay here," he told Scooter and the boys, "I'm going to ask some of the dock workers if they had seen them."

"Alright," Scooter agreed.

Joey turned to Roc and Ks, "Come on, Rocks," he urged.

Joey headed to the ship, with the rocks following behind. He saw a crewmember unloading a few crates from the ship. He walked up to him and tapped him on the shoulder.

"Excuse me, sir," he said, "I would like to ask you a question."

The crewmember turned around and set a crate down. He moved a toothpick in his mouth.

"Aye," he replied, "What can I do for ya?"

"Was there a fellow name Mr. Gregory on this ship?"

"Aye."

"How long ago was that?"

"Oh, he's been gone for o'er an hour now," the crew member said, "The man travels quickly, you know. Doe'nt stop for no one, not even the devil h'mself."

"Do you know where he is heading?"

"Yea, I think. I overheard he was goin' to the bank to finish some financial business of his. After that, he said he would be goin' to some apartments, now what did he call he 'em? Somber at the Kaleidoscope? Slumber at the..."

"Sonder at the Vitascope?" Joey interjected, hopefully.

"Aye, that was the spot!"

"Thank you, sir," Joey said, nodding to the gentleman. He and the rocks sprinted back to Scooter and the boys.

"They left about an hour ago," Joey panted, "Mr. Gregory went to the Sonder at the Vitascope, an apartment building. If we hurry, we can make it there before he leaves."

"Okay," said Scooter, energetically, "Let's do this, boys!"

"You guys go ahead to the mansion. Stick to the plan!" Joey explained, "The rocks and I will follow Mr. Gregory."

"Right, we'll have your friends rescued in no time, Joey" Ricky said.

"Yep," Tommy Lee agreed, "No one will be held hostage here, or my name ain't Tommy Lee!"

The three boys waved down a taxi and headed toward the mansion.

Joey turned to the rocks, "You ready?"

"Of course, we've been ready this whole trip," Roc said,"

Joey picked up his suitcase, "Let's go then."

****

A dark, navy-blue cab slowly came to a stop outside of the Sonder at the Vitascope, an apartment building with several stories. The driver parked the car and got out. He went to the passenger door and held it open for Mr. Gregory, who stepped out, stretched, and sighed. *Time to get this over with*, he thought to himself. He walked inside the building and headed to the reception desk. A woman behind the desk was typing away on her computer. She looked up and gasped.

"Mr. Woods, sir, what can I do for you?"

"I'm here to visit my relatives," Mr. Gregory answered.

"Yes sir," she replied, "Level 3, room number 5."

"Thank you, ma'am," Mr. Gregory said with a tip of his hat.

He walked to the elevator and pressed the button to level 3. The doors opened and revealed the 3rd story. He read the room's number plates until he reached number 5. Taking his hat off, he took a deep breath and rang the doorbell. The door opened slightly, and a young woman's face peered through the slit. Upon realizing who it was, she opened the door wide with a smile.

"Hello uncle," she said in happy tone, "Come in."

"Thank you, Ruth," said Mr. Gregory.

She stepped aside to let him walk in. His older teenage nephew came out of the bedroom. He had on a white dress shirt, a red tie, and black dress pants. He stopped in his tracks when he saw Mr. Gregory.

"Uncle Gregory," he said respectfully, "Thanks for coming!"

"It's good to see you again, Smith," Mr. Gregory said, shaking his hand, "What's it's like being the head of the house while your father is overseas?"

"It can be hard sometimes," Smith answered, "But it's a learning experience."

"That's good, it'll teach you how to be a man."

Smith nodded, "I'll take you to Mother."

Smith walked briskly down the hall as he led Mr. Gregory to the living room. Inside the room, Mrs. Woods sat on a sofa reading a book. She wore a vibrant green dress, and her red hair was tied back in a bun with curls hanging around her face. Nearby, two little brown-haired girls played cards on the floor. They looked up when Mr. Gregory, Ruth, and Smith entered the room.

"Hello uncle!" the two girls chimed, jumping to their feet.

"Why, hello Amy, Haley," Mr. Gregory grinned.

The mother sat down her book, stood up quickly and walked over to Mr. Gregory. Mrs. Woods was tall for a woman, and Mr. Gregory was shorter than your

average man. The height difference between the two was readily apparent.

"Gregory," she said, giving him a hug, "It's good to see you again!"

"You too, Irene" Mr. Gregory replied, "I've been very busy the last few weeks tending to my…er…business."

"What kind of business?" Ruth asked.

"It's not important really, it would bore the life out of all of you."

Mrs. Woods nodded, "We won't pry then. Let me get you a glass of tea," she said.

Mrs. Woods retreated to the kitchen and fetched some tea. Mr. Gregory sat on the sofa and accepted the cup of tea she had handed to him. Mrs. Woods sat down on the rocker next to the sofa. Mr. Gregory drank the tea in big gulps. He set the cup on the table with a clang, smacking his lips.

"How's everything going at the mansion?" asked Mrs. Woods.

"Oh," Mr. Gregory mumbled, "I haven't begun renovation yet. The contractors are giving me a hard time."

"Why?"

"Oh, you know these business types, always fooling around," Mr. Gregory replied, "Also, it's going to take an enormous sum to repair the heavy damage from Hurricane Ida."

"Oh, I'm sorry," said Mrs. Woods, lowering her head. "Yes…Ida did a lot more damage than it should've." Mrs.

Woods sat silent for a moment before speaking again, "Everything seemed to turn against us." The kids had a sad look on their faces also.

"Well," said Mr. Gregory, "I will try the best to my ability to get it back in shape. Ivan trusted me to fix the mansion, and that's what I intend to do. But, as I said, it will take a while before it is habitable again, maybe six to seven months, if that. It really is in bad condition."

"Alright," Mrs. Woods sighed. She then added, "How did the quest for the cat statue turn out?"

"Very well, in fact, I have it with me right now."

He picked up his suitcase, opened the case, and turned it around to show everyone. The family's eyes lit up with wonder. Amy and Haley reached out and poked at the statue.

"So, this is the one that has the rubies?" asked Smith, his eyes not leaving the statue.

"In theory, yes," Mr. Gregory pointed out, "We already collected a Ruby Cat with a X, but when we broke it open, the rubies weren't inside. So, someone had a false X written on the bottom of the statue to fool other collectors, like me. But we believe this statue is genuine, and I will inspect it further when I get back to the mansion."

"Let's hope it's the real one," Mrs. Wood said, leaning back in her chair, "When will you be leaving for the mansion?"

"Right now, actually," Mr. Gregory answered, looking at his watch, "I must be going. Thanks for the tea, Irene."

"It was a pleasure to see you again," Mrs. Woods replied, rising from her chair to walk him to the front door.

****

Joey pulled his ear away from the door. He looked at Roc and Ks, "Did you hear that, rocks?" he whispered, "Mr. Gregory is telling these people a whole different story than what is actually going on! This must be the Woods family."

****

Mrs. Woods and the kids bid him farewell at the door.

"Goodbye, uncle," the four kids said in unison.

"Goodbye, children," Mr. Gregory replied. He looked at Mrs. Woods.

"You'll keep us updated, won't you?" she asked.

"I will try," he said, "Goodbye, Irene."

He left the apartment and walked down to the elevator and got on. Mrs. Woods sighed and stepped back into her apartment. Joey and the rocks peeked through the slightly ajar door of the janitor's closet in the hallway. The coast was clear. Joey crept out of the closet with the rocks following.

"Alright, rocks," said Joey, as they reached the elevator, "so now we know who used to own the house."

"And we also know why it's named *"Woods' Mansion"*," Ks explained, "It wasn't because of the acres of woods around the mansion."

"It's because of the Woods family; it's their ancestral estate," Roc concluded.

"Right," Joey agreed. "We need to hurry back; our friends will need help."

Joey opened the elevator and he and the rocks walked inside. He pushed the button to the first floor. The rocks did a little snapping of their fingers to the catchy tune that was playing. As the elevator doors slid open, Joey peeked from side to side, making sure Mr. Gregory was not still in the lobby. He looked out the main entrance doors just as Mr. Gregory's cab pulled away. He motioned for the rocks to follow him outside, but suddenly he froze in his tracks. The rocks bumped into him.

"Hey!" Roc and Ks exclaimed, "What's the hold up?"

"Wait," he told the rocks, staring into the distance. He snapped his fingers and smiled, "I have another idea, stay here."

Roc and Ks shrugged to each other as Joey ran back into the elevator. He jabbed his thumb into the 3rd level button and waited. As soon as the doors opened, he briskly walked down to the Woods' room and rang the bell. Hopefully, his new plan would succeed.

Chapter 14: Breaching the Fortress

The sky's bright pink color reflected off the plaque that hung on the gates of the Woods' Mansion. Scooter peeked through the gates and scanned the area. Parked in front of the mansion was the van that held Radford and the family. Two men stood guard near the mansion's door. Scooter looked around the perimeter of the house for another way to get in. On the eastern face of the mansion, Scooter noticed a cellar hatch against the wall. He motioned for the boys to come over.

"Look," he whispered, "There's a cellar hatch on the left side of the building. If we use the forest to hide, we can sneak around the mansion and get in through the cellar."

"Right," the boys agreed.

The three boys ran along the outside wall to the wooded part of the mansion's grounds. Tommy Lee and Ricky then got on their knees and cupped their hands together. Scooter stepped up on their hands and the boys gave him a boost up to the ledge of the wall. Scooter hoisted himself onto the wall, keeping a low profile. The coast was clear. Tommy Lee crouched low and let Ricky use his back as a step. Scooter reached down and pulled Ricky up on the wall, and together they pulled Tommy Lee up. They jumped to the ground quietly and crept through the woods towards the mansion. They saw the two guards were still standing at the front door.

The mosquitoes swarming around the three boys combined with the muggy evening made it nearly impossible to stand still.

"Keep a low profile," Scooter whispered, swatting a mosquito on his cheek, "If they start walking towards you, throw a stick or something away from you to distract them.

Climbing out of the brush, Scooter dove behind a tree and peeked around the rough bark. The men were in a deep conversation, oblivious to the boys sneaking around the trees. Scooter turned to the boys and motioned for them to come over. Ricky and Tommy Lee crept through the brush, following Scooter's trail. Suddenly, a small twig snapped underneath Ricky's foot. One of the guards at the door, with a turn of his heel, looked over at the wooded area.

"What was that!?" he exclaimed, drawing his handgun.

Scooter gulped. These men were armed.

"What was what?" sighed the second guard, barely turning his head.

"I heard something snap in the forest," the guard said, alarmed, "Someone's out there!"

"Bah, John," yawned the second guard, "You're just hearing things."

"I swear I heard something," the first guard said, stuffing his gun back into his belt.

Scooter and the boys peaked out from behind the trees, breathing heavily. They couldn't afford to get captured twice in one adventure. They crept out from behind the trees towards the cellar again. Tommy Lee nudged Scooter in the arm and pointed frantically to a fenced caged near the mansion. Two massive pit bulls slumbered in their kennels. A chill shot up Scooter's spine, and he quickly put a finger to his mouth. If they woke the dogs, they would be dead ducks. Sneaking by the dogs as quietly as their fear allowed, they made it to the cellar doors, just as the sun disappeared below the horizon. The sky was now a dark azure blue, and the moon had begun its ascent, peeking over the horizon.

Scooter turned to the boys. "Alright, we're gonna sneak inside and get Radford and the Abels out of there," he whispered, "Stick to the plan, get in, grab our friends, and get out."

"And don't get caught," Ricky added.

Scooter slowly opened the wooden doors, which, owing to the rusted hinges, creaked slightly. A stairway led down into the cellar, poorly lit by only a few electric lamps hanging from wires. Scooter silently walked down the steps and looked around the cellar. A few crates, barrels of wine, and boxes of rotting roots lined the walls. A leaky sprinkler system stretched across the ceiling. Although underground, the cellar was quite spacious. The other boys tiptoed down the steps, with Tommy Lee quietly closing the cellar door behind them.

"This is a pretty cool cellar," Tommy Lee said, looking around, "Almost seems like a bunker."

A corkscrew flight of stairs led upwards to a wooden hatch in the ceiling. Scooter climbed the stairs and pushed up on the door above his head. The door moved. Opening the door slightly and quietly, he peeked through the crack. The door to the cellar they were in was hidden underneath a rug inside a room. Scooter couldn't make out which room it was, but he saw pool cues lined against the wall. He assumed it was a billiard room. Scooter crawled out and held the door open for the boys, who climbed out one after the other. After everyone was out of the cellar, Scooter carefully shut the door and placed the rug back over it. It turned out that Scooter was correct; they were in an old billiard room, evident by the massive, dust-caked billiard table in the center of the room. The secret door was hidden under a rug near a tall window.

Scooter whispered to the boys. "Alright Tommy Lee, come with me. Ricky, stay here and wait for us. If someone comes into this room, hide yourself and don't move a hair."

"Okay dude," replied Ricky, "Try to hurry though, it's creeping me out down here."

Scooter and Tommy Lee quietly left the billiard room and tiptoed down the dilapidated hall. It had a red, ragged, wool rug that ran the length of it. The hall intersected the front entrance of the house, and the duo peeked around the corner. Three men were talking to each other by the big front doors. Suddenly, the doorbell rang, and the men quickly stopped chattering and stood ready to greet their guest. A man in a vest, who Scooter assumed was the butler, appeared and opened the door. The boss himself came in, Mr. Gregory. Scooter and Tommy Lee gasped, and they ducked back into the hall. Scooter dove behind a bookshelf, and Tommy Lee clambered inside an enormous ern. Mr. Gregory walked by with his men and butler following behind.

"And what do we do with the hostages, sir?" the butler asked.

"Give them some water and food," he replied, I don't want them fainting on us. We may take hostages, but we aren't savages."

"Yes, sir," said the butler monotonously, and he headed to the kitchen.

Mr. Gregory and the other three men entered an office at the end of the hall and closed the door. Scooter and Tommy climbed out of their hiding spots and huddled together.

"Let's follow the butler," Scooter whispered to Tommy, "He's going to bring food to Radford and the Abels, so he will bring us right to them."

They followed the butler to the kitchen and waited out in the hall for him to finish preparing the food. The butler came out with a big platter containing plates of cheese and crackers and a jug of water. He headed to the hostage's room.

Scooter started to follow the butler from behind and motioned for Tommy Lee, but Tommy Lee was nowhere to be seen.

"Tommy!" whispered Scooter, "Where the heck are you?"

Tommy Lee snuck out of the kitchen, eating a fluffy biscuit.

"What?" asked Tommy with a mouthful of biscuit, "It's free food!"

"Idiot! How'd you even get in there?!" Scooter scolded.

Tommy Lee shrugged. Scooter rolled his eyes and they both moved along quietly to keep up with the butler.

The butler came to the door of yet another room. When he opened it, the two boys could see that it was an old bedroom, with a 19th century look, and a Victorian styled bunk bed. There were tables, drawers and chairs all in an advanced state of decay. The butler entered the room and set the plater on a small round table. Radford and the Abels looked up.

"The master ordered me to give you some food," the butler said, setting out the plates, "Eat now."

"How long will you hold us here?" Radford demanded, rising out of his chair.

"I don't know," the butler shrugged, "I don't know what Mr. Gregory wants. He may want to keep you as hostages for ransom."

"One thing's for sure," Radford told him, "Our friends will look for us, but they won't pay you a penny to get us back."

"It is not my doing, sir," the butler said, picking up the platter, "I only follow my master's orders."

Without another word, he left the room and locked the door, hiding the key in a cabinet near the door. He walked back to the kitchen. Scooter and Tommy Lee crept out of a closet they were hiding in and ran to the drawer the butler hid the key in. Scooter rifled through the drawers while Tommy Lee kept watch. Scooter's finger hit something smooth and hard, the key! He quickly shut the drawer and hurried to the door. He jammed the key into the lock, turning it back and forth until he heard "click". He opened the door and sighed in relief. They were all right there, together. Radford gasped and ran to Scooter, giving him a big hug.

"Scooter, my boy," he whispered, thumping his back, "How did you find us?"

"We followed the butler when he was bringing you food," Scooter answered, wheezing, "We found a cellar with a secret door that leads to the billiard room. Ricky is in the room now and Tommy Lee is in the hall, both keeping watch."

"Great!" Bert and Alice cried, and they began to run out of the room, "Let's go!"

"Wait!" Scooter grabbed the children's arms, "We need to take you guys out in pairs. If we all go, we're sure to be caught instantly. I'll take your grandparents and Radford out first, and then we will come back for you two and your parents. Also, just in case one of Mr. Gregory's men, or himself, comes back before we return, place pillows underneath the bed sheets to look like the grandparents could be sleeping. Do the same to the top bunk to make it look like Radford is sleeping."

"Okay," the family agreed, and got right to work arranging the pillows under the covers.

Scooter led Radford and the Abels' grandparents out of the room. Radford saw Tommy Lee and shook his hand, and Tommy led them to the billiard room. Ricky waited for them at the cellar doors and helped the grandparents down the stairs. He turned to Radford.

"There's a spiral staircase that leads to the cellar's floor," he whispered, "At the far end of the cellar, beyond the wine barrels, there is a door that leads outside. Be careful though, there are watchdogs close by in cages. They were asleep, but if you wake those monsters, the whole operation is a bust."

"Thank you," Radford said, "We'll be careful," and headed down the stairs with the grandparents.

Ricky closed the secret door and returned to his hiding spot. Tommy Lee headed back to the bedroom. When he returned, the disguise "dummies" were already in place.

"How does it look?" Bert asked.

"Realistic enough," Scooter answered, who had stayed behind to help, "They'll have to do. Let's hurry now, Radford and your grandparents are already outside. Let's get outta here."

✳✳✳✳✳✳✳✳✳✳✳✳✳✳✳✳✳

Mr. Gregory sat down in a worn, leather desk chair in the dingy office. He wondered how he would get the troublemakers to pay the ransom for his hostages. A new problem then hit him smack square in the face.

"I just realized," he said to Ardanan, "Even if we keep those folks here until we find the rubies, they're going tell the police anyway about our whereabouts."

"I hate to break it to you, boss," Ardanan said, "But you got a member of the police with you. That man with the glasses and round hat is Radford Weston, a senior police detective."

"What!?" Mr. Gregory exclaimed, "Why on earth didn't you tell me that sooner?"

"I assumed you knew already, he's quite famous here in New Orleans."

"Well, I thought he looked familiar, I just couldn't tell for sure. Curse it! If we let them go, the entire police force would be on our backs in minutes." Mr. Gregory slumped back in his chair.

"We could just make them disappear permanently," Ardanan muttered.

"No," Mr. Gregory sighed, "we aren't using your underworld methods here. That would create more problems than it solves."

"As you wish," Ardanan shrugged.

Mr. Gregory got out of his chair and strutted to the door, "Come on, let's try to figure this out. I just need those rubies, that's the main priority."

****

Scooter led the procession towards the billiard room. As they were creeping down the hall, the office door abruptly opened, and out came Mr. Gregory and his men! The two groups locked eyes for a split second.

Mr. Gregory snapped out of his shock and shouted. "GET THEM!"

"Hurry, hurry!" Scooter yelled, pushing the family faster, "Get into the billiard room!"

Mr. Gregory's men broke into a full run and chased them down the hall. Scooter burst into the billiard room and shouted to Ricky.

"Open the door, hurry! We've been spotted!"

Ricky threw back the rug and fumbled with the latch, "Shucks, open up bro!" He finally swung the door open. "Get in!" he shouted.

Bert and Alice tumbled down the steps first, followed by their parents. Only Scooter and the boys were left.

"Stop right there!" a voice boomed, "And you four come out of that cellar, or we'll shoot your friends!"

They turned around and saw the two men at the door with derringers in their hands. Scooter and the boys raised their hands, and the family slowly climbed out of the cellar. Mr. Gregory burst into the room, panting and furious.

"What do you think you are doing!?" he roared.

"Sorry, sir," Scooter retaliated, arms crossed "But you have no right to hold someone against their will. Just let us alone and we won't call the police."

Mr. Gregory started laughing. "How do I know you won't report me to the police, huh?" he gasped, chuckling, "Your friend in the glasses is a cop!"

"No, sir, we won't say anything" Mr. Klaus told him, "We just want to leave this place."

"Okay…I see how it has to be," Mr. Gregory said, pointing a finger at the group, "If you say one word of this to the police…I'll kill you all."

"What!?" the family exclaimed, "You can't be serious!"

"Do you really think I'm playing with you?" Mr. Gregory scoffed. He looked at Radford, "You dare tell any of this to your chief, old man, and I will kill you. I don't care if you're a cop."

He turned to the Abels, "I'm telling you straight up, I kill you if you tell the law about this. I know where you live."

"But this family just wants to go home," Scooter insisted, forgetting himself, "You can't threaten them with death!"

"I don't care about any of that family stuff," Mr. Gregory snorted, "Why, I even lied to my own family to steal this mansion from them!"

"That will be all, Mr. Gregory, that's all we need" a voice boomed from behind him.

Mr. Gregory's face turned white as a sheet. He slowly turned around and saw right before him the chief of the New Orleans Police, Chief Anderson himself! He was a broad shouldered, massive man, with a bushy blond beard and a gruff voice. Joey and Officers Eric Garrison and

Nathan Richards stood beside him. Officer Richards held the two men at gunpoint, while Garrison took the derringers from their hands. Mr. Gregory stumbled back, beginning to stutter.

"Uh…Chief…I-I didn't mean what I said…I was only trying to scare these thieves."

"You know full well that's not true," Chief Anderson told him, with his arms behind his back, "You and your men are under arrest."

"You are playing games with me," Mr. Gregory shuddered, "Under what charges?"

"For one," the chief said, pointing to the Abels, "Makin death threats and threatening with a firearm."

"Oh…t-these are the thieves I just told you about," Mr. Gregory mumbled, looking for an excuse. "I was just going to let them leave if they would get off my land."

"Liar!" Bert and Alice screamed, "You were only going to let us leave if we didn't say a word!"

"And you were keeping our friends here from rescuing us," Mr. Klaus added in, "Threatening us and them with death to keep us silenced!"

Mr. Gregory a menacing look at the family, who glared at him in return. Chief Anderson ordered Richards to take a few officers with him and search the house. They were to find the rest of Mr. Gregory's clan and arrest them. He then ordered the butler to lead the police throughout the house. Chief Anderson returned his gaze to Mr. Gregory.

"Also, my detective here believes you've swindled this mansion from its rightful owners. We will investigate that as well."

"I did no such thing!" Mr. Gregory protested, "My relatives willing gave me the mansion, fair and square! Why, they didn't even care to have this place anymore!"

"Ah yes," Joey spoke up, "about that. I brought the Woods here myself, to remind you of the little chat you had with them. I just so happened to be there, and I told them everything I know. They were quite shocked to hear that you wanted to turn their mansion into a museum."

Mrs. Woods and her kids stepped into the room. Mrs. Woods had a long, sad look on her face. Mr. Gregory looked paler than ever.

"You never told us you wanted this mansion for a museum," Mrs. Woods said in a firm voice, "You lied to us about fixing this mansion. You never once told us you were keeping it for yourself."

"And in addition to all of that," Chief Anderson added, "You stole a family treasure from the Abels, and shattered it before their very eyes." He paused, pulled a piece of paper out of his pocket, and read it.

"One more thing," he continued," The mysterious home invasions that had my men bamboozled for weeks were your doings as well. You ordered your thugs to ransack honest people's homes in search of the Ruby Cat. That is another added charge to your roster."

Mr. Gregory was at a loss for words. The accusations were true, and everyone knew it. Officer Garrison took out his handcuffs and locked them on Mr. Gregory's wrists. Officer Garrison began to lead Mr. Gregory out of the room and read him his Miranda rights, when, abruptly, the front doors in the lobby slammed open. They heard footsteps running up to the billiard room at a quick pace, and then, in burst Ardanan.

"Boss," he said breathing heavily, "The cops are all over…." He froze, seeing his boss in handcuffs and the police standing right there. He turned his head and saw the butler and the police officers rounding up the rest of his gang. Turning on his heel, he bolted to the front door.

"Someone, stop that man!" Chief Anderson shouted.

"Don't worry, Chief," Joey said, taking of in a full run, "I'll get him!"

Ardanan ran through the front doors with Joey hot on his heels. Ardanan knew he couldn't lose Joey running across the long driveway, so he took off into the forest.

Radford and the grandparents had just emerged from the cellar when Ardanan and Joey bolted past them into the forest. The dogs in the kennel howled. A shiver shot up Radford's spine; it was too dark for him to realize it was Joey in pursuit of Ardanan.

"If I was superstitious man, I might believe these woods are haunted." he shuddered.

Ardanan pushed through a thick, springy bough and let it lash out behind him. Joey saw the branch swinging towards him, but he dove to the ground as the branch swung just over his head. Joey scrambled to his feet and began to run full speed once more. Ardanan growled and ran at a faster pace. Up ahead, a huge log obstructed their path. Ardanan hurdled over the log with a mighty leap.

Joey hurdled over the log as well, but his foot slipped on some leaves, and he bit the dust. He spit out the dirt, regained his footing, and started running again.

"Curses!" Ardanan shouted.

He looked up and saw the wall that surrounded the entire mansion's park was just ahead. If he could just climb over the walls, he would be free!

"Give up, Ardanan!" Joey exclaimed, "The game's over!"

"Never!" Ardanan shouted back, "You ain't taking me back to prison!" He turned his sight to the wall again.

However, for no apparent reason, his heels flipped out from beneath him. *Poof!* He landed face first in the dust. Joey ran up to the scene with a big grin on his face.

"Ha! Good job, Rocks!" he exclaimed.

Roc and Ks picked themselves up and dusted off.

"Yeah," Roc explained, "When you told us to stay outside and watch for anyone trying to escape; that was a great idea."

"We heard all the commotion and deducted the ruffian would run to the forest," Ks added, "It's only obvious that any villain would dash to the forest to escape the police."

"Splendid!" Joey said as he walked over to Ardanan with his cuffs, "That's some great detective thinking right there."

Ardanan lifted his face out of the dirt, spitting out some grit. "Ugh, yuck!" he said. Joey slapped the cuffs on his wrists and hauled him to his feet.

"Look at his face!" laughed Ks, pointing at Ardanan. Joey and Roc looked at Ardanan and wheezed, trying to hold back their laughter. Ardanan's face was caked with dirt and dead grass.

"Looks like we gave him a 'face plant,'" Roc grinned.

The three howled with laughter as they brought their captive back to the mansion, while the moon shone brightly overhead.

Chapter 15: The Grand Opening

Ping! Ping! Joey had been carving away the cat statue for a few minutes now with a chisel and hammer. He was using extreme caution, taking care not to chip the rubies in the process. That is, if there were any rubies; he didn't want to take any chances. The table in his apartment room was covered in dust from the now disfigured Ruby Cat. The light fixture hanging above shone down on the table, providing light needed for the task. Scooter, Radford, the boys, and the Abel family stood around him, watching with wide eyes, hypnotized. The statue was becoming smaller and smaller. Now came the most difficult part, carving around something of great value that might, or not, be there in the first place. Joey began to sweat; he wiped his brow and removed his coat before getting back to work. He placed the chisel on the statue and began lightly tapping again. Suddenly, the chisel hit an object of harder material than the statue's porcelain.

"There's something hard in here!" Joey said excitedly to the group who stood around the table. Roc and Ks, who had been standing nearby, climbed onto the table to watch closer. Joey brushed the dust off the hard material and froze. The hard material had a rich black color underneath the pale yellow-grey statue. He tapped the statue again. *Crack!* The remaining bit of the statue fell in two pieces from Joey's hands onto the table. Two marble shaped spheres bounced out of the statue and rolled off the table. Joey swooped down and quickly snatched up the two objects in his hand before they hit the floor. He slowly stood to his feet, a huge smile on his face. He opened his hand very slowly and the light from above shone down on his hands. A vibrant, red color glistened out of the spheres in his hands, the rubies. The perfectly cut jewels were a sight to their travel-weary eyes. Joey held them up for everyone to see.

"The…the rubies!?" the rocks stammered, "Those are the rubies!?"

Joey smiled again and nodded his head. Bert and Alice moved in closer and stared at the rubies, awestruck.

"May we hold them?" Bert asked.

Joey carefully placed a ruby into each of the kids' hands. They gazed at the thimble-sized rubies with wide eyes for a few seconds, and then handed them to Ricky and Tommy Lee. The boys were amazed and at the same time in disbelief of what they were holding.

"This doesn't seem real, man," Ricky said in amazement.

"I know bro," Tommy agreed, "It feels like a dream."

After they had their few seconds of administration, they handed them to the rest of the Abels. The passing of the gems around the room continued until everyone had a good look at the rubies. The last to receive the rubies were Radford and Scooter. Radford repeatedly lowered and lifted his glasses.

"Marvelous!" he said, turning the ruby over in his hand, "These are masterpieces of jewelry craft. The face is intricately cut. And the color, it is such a stunningly rich red."

They carefully handed them back to Joey. Joey took out a little felt bag from his coat and dropped the rubies in it, cinching the bag's drawstring tight. He put the bag into his desk's drawer and looked at the clock.

"Why, it's almost 11:00," Joey said, checking his watch too. He turned to the Abels, "We better get you guys to the airport on time, or you will miss your flight back to Berlin."

Mr. and Mrs. Abel looked at the clock and gasped, "Oh my," Mr. Klaus said, grabbing his suitcase, "We better be on our way!"

****

The pilots started up the massive jumbo jet's engines in preparation for take-off. The loudspeakers in the airport alerted all passengers that the 11:00 o'clock morning flight was boarding. All the passengers began to pick up their suitcases and walked towards the gate. They were prepared for the long flight back to Europe.

Mr. Klaus shook Joey's hand. "Well, it's time to say goodbye, friend," he said with a smile, "We are going to miss all of you."

Mrs. Maria shook each of their hands vigorously, "Thank you, sirs, for all your kindness to us."

"No problem, ma'am," said Radford, "We are honored to help."

Mr. Klaus came to Tommy Lee and Ricky and shook their hands, "Thanks, friends. Stay safe out there."

Tommy grinned, "We will, sir, and you as well!"

"See ya laters, dude!" Ricky said.

Mr. Klaus shook Scooter's hand as well, "Goodbye sir, we'll always remember your bravery when you tried to rescue us."

"Thanks, sir," Scooter grinned.

The grandmother and grandfather shook Joey and Radford's hands as well, followed by Scooter and the boys.

"Bless you, sirs, for your generosity," the grandmother said.

Bert and Alice began to say their goodbyes.

"Goodbye, sirs," Bert said, "We will miss you. It was nice to meet you all."

Alice had a sad look on her face, "Bye, I will miss you all."

"We will as well, children," Radford smiled, "You all be careful back home."

Joey reached down to grab his suitcase when he felt something in his coat pocket. He pulled it out and found it was the trinket Bert and Alice had given him earlier. He decided to give it back, he didn't need it anymore. Then he stopped; nor did the family need it anymore. Looking around at all the happy, laughing faces, Joey knew that they had put their trust in Spiritual assurance, instead of physical. He slid the trinket back into his pocket and opened his suitcase, pulling out another relic, a cat statue.

"Here," he explained, handing it to Mr. Klaus, "It is a copy of one of the cat statues at the Woods' mansion. The Woods agreed you should have it. It may not be exactly like the one you had but it's very close."

Mr. Klaus gently took the statue with gratitude, "Thank you. We will treasure this statue as if it was our own."

Mr. Klaus leaned over to Radford and Joey, "Also, we found the Watchmaker last night and invited Him in," he nodded.

"Wonderful, my man!" Radford beamed.

"Watchmaker?" Joey asked in confusion, "I didn't see any watchmaker back in Berlin."

"*The* Watchmaker," Radford replied with a wink.

"Ah," Joey grinned, "I see now. Good to hear."

The family turned their heads to the rocks.

"Goodbye, Roc and Ks," Mr. Klaus said, "You two look after the folks, okay?"

"Don't worry, sir," Roc stated, "We have been looking out for these guys for years now."

The family left the airport and headed to the plane that was going to take them back to Berlin. In a few minutes, the plane began to speed down the runway. That was the last time Joey and his friends saw the Abels' faces as the plane flew into the air, disappearing behind the clouds.

After leaving the airport, it was time for Ricky and Tommy Lee to say their goodbyes.

"Well, dudes," said Ricky, breathing in the fresh air, "My bro and I better start heading home now. What strange coincidences that we would be on the exact same adventure and meet up at the exact same time in Berlin."

"Yep," Tommy Lee agreed, "It beats all odds."

"I guess we will be seeing each other again soon," Joey assumed, "You live around Canal Street?"

"Yes sir," Ricky affirmed, "We live a couple blocks from there. We plan to be at the museum's grand opening tomorrow."

"Ah, great," Joey exclaimed, "Well see you there then!"

"See ya!" The boys said, and then they looked at the rocks.

"Goodbye you two," Tommy Lee smiled, "What crazy freaks you are!"

"Yeah," agreed Ricky as he shot the peace sign, "Peace little dudes!"

"See you around," replied Roc and Ks. As they walked away, Ks hollered, "Don't forget to wear nice clothes! This isn't your average get-together, remember?"

"Don't you worry," the boys reassured, "We won't forget!"

The rocks turned to Joey with big grins on their faces. "Now, time to cash in those rubies!" Ks exclaimed.

Joey thought about the large amount of cash they would get; it would be a nice financial buffer. He sighed with a grin and shook his head. "Nah rocks, we aren't going to cash it in, I have a better idea."

"Wait…what!?" the rocks asked bewildered.

"You'll see tomorrow, guys," Joey replied, "But for now, it's time for a well-earned rest."

****

A large crowd had gathered in the street in front of the new museum. They were all dressed rather well for the opening ceremony of the New Orleans's Museum, which had recently finished construction. Chief Anderson of the New Orleans Police Department and a few council members gathered on the steps of the museum, with a microphone on the podium placed in front of them. The mayor of New Orleans was there as well; ready to give his speech. Joey, Radford, and the rocks were also present. The rocks, wearing their ties, beamed thinking they looked quite sophisticated.

The mayor walked up to the podium and thumped on the microphone. The crowd grew silent.

"Good evening, ladies and gentlemen," the mayor boomed, "welcome as we gather to celebrate the opening of the Hoffman and Thornwell's Museum of Natural History. First, we would like to thank the following gentlemen who made this possible: Professor Ronald Trojan, from the University of New Orleans, fossil exhibit, Professor Ferdinand Nickel, from the Tulane University, archeology and human history exhibits, and Professor Parratus P. Eye, from Xavier University of Louisiana, aquatics and wildlife exhibit. Also, our appreciation to our architect Mr. David Brown, who designed the museum's beautiful layout. And finally, thanks to Detectives Packard and Weston, who made a special display case of the mysterious and legendary Ruby Cat, located in the main hall of the museum. Now, without further ado, let's cut the ribbon."

The mayor stepped away from the microphone and an assistant handed him the giant, gold scissors. The mayor stepped up to the red ribbon and with one snip, cut the ribbon. The crowd cheered. The doors of the museum swung open, and the people swarmed in. Joey, the rocks, and Radford headed to their glass exhibit with the Ruby Cat and rubies inside. A red velvet cloth covered the glass case as a rather large crowd gathered around. Joey stepped up to the glass case.

"The items underneath this case weren't easy to obtain," he announced to the crowd, "We had to travel all the way to Europe and back to obtain what you are about to see."

Joey pulled back the cloth with one swift motion, and the crowd murmured with excitement. A ceramic cat statue, a replica of the real ruby cat, placed atop a beautiful display, was polished, and shone in the sun, which streamed in through the overhead windows. The rubies, placed atop two fancy stands, shimmered. The crowd pressed close around the case, trying to take pictures of the fantastic display. Joey struggled through the crowd to head back to Radford and the rocks. Scooter, Ricky, and Tommy Lee appeared out of the crowd, and joined the four.

"Well, how about that, guys?" Joey said enthusiastically, "We found the rubies, helped the Woods find out the truth about their estate, and we have contributed a valuable piece of history to our museum. All's well that ends well."

"Yeah, dude, that phrase definitely has a place here," Ricky smiled. "And I'm glad."

"I will be paying you two a cut of the money you would've gotten from the rubies," Joey told Ricky and Tommy Lee, "It'll just take a bit of time to get it all in."

"Don't rush it, we can wait. We published our video last night," Tommy Lee added, "The views are already pouring in by the thousands as we speak! We will be fine until you get the money."

Joey nodded and turned to the rocks, "And isn't this better than cashing the rubies in?"

"You're right," Roc said, "It's better seeing people's faces light up than having a few more bucks stuffed into our pockets."

"Undoubtedly," Radford agreed, "Now, let's check out these exhibits!"

The friends grabbed some coffee from the museum's cafe and headed to the exhibits, enjoying themselves after a job well done.

Chapter 16: Wrapping It All Up

It had been a month since the opening of the Hoffman and Thornwell's Museum Natural History. Joey, Roc, and Ks walked to the front gates of "*Mansion of the Woods.*" and rang the bell. The gatekeeper opened the gates, and they entered the large park of the mansion. Workers were scattered throughout the park and mansion, carrying out the renovations.

"Why, the mansion looks amazing today!" he exclaimed in awe, breathing in the fresh air.

"Absolutely," Ks agreed, "The renovations has come along nicely!"

"So let me get this straight," Roc asked, "Mrs. Woods senior left the mansion with her two boys, Ivan and Gregory, after her husband had died. The mansion fell into disrepair after a few decades. Eventually, Ivan, the eldest son and heir, decided to return to the mansion and fix it up. He was now a grown man with a family of his own. However, being a communications officer in the Army, he was deployed overseas just as the renovations began, and Hurricane Ida damaged the mansion even further. So then…how did Gregory get it again?"

"Mr. Gregory concocted a fraudulent plan to take the mansion while Ivan was away. He forged a deed with the homeowner's name, in this case Ivan's." Joey explained, "He covered his tracks by saying he would be repairing the mansion. By saying this he did not arouse Mr. and Mrs. Woods' suspicion while he was 'fixing' the mansion. Mr. and Mrs. Woods would pay him for the work, but he would oversee the renovations. He wanted the mansion to be turned into his museum so he could compete against Hoffman and Thornwell's Museum of Natural History. Either it was solely just him wanting the fame and glory, or there was some bad blood between the two behind closed doors."

"Ah, I see," Roc said, "Bet it would be painful to find out your own brother swindled you out of your home."

"Yep, it turned into to a lengthy legal battle, but it appears they got the mansion back."

They walked up to the two giant front doors and rang the bell. After a few seconds of waiting, the butler opened the door.

"Good evening, Mr. Packard," the butler said clasping his hands together, "I hope your day is fine."

"It sure is, Barney," Joey replied, "How are the Woods?"

"They are doing very well sir," Barney replied, "The family is expecting you."

He stepped back and let Joey and the rocks enter. He then led them down the long hall of the mansion to the living room. Butler Barney opened the living room door and directed Joey into the room with the motion of his hand. He spoke up to get the attention of the family. The family was well dressed in fine clothes.

"Mr. Packard and the rocks are here to visit," Barney announced.

Mrs. Woods and her kids smiled in delight and rushed to the door.

"Hello, Joey! Hello Rocks!" the little girls exclaimed in harmony.

"Why, hello Mr. Packard," Mrs. Woods said, giving him a vigorous handshake. "How have you been?"

"I've been doing well, Mrs. Woods," Joey replied, "Ks, Roc, and I are here to see how you are doing and how the renovations are coming along."

"We are doing very well, thank you," Mrs. Woods informed him, "My boy Smith is out at the moment, and he won't be here until later. Anyhow, let me show you around the mansion. As you saw, we are nearing completion with the renovations."

Mrs. Woods walked out into the hall and Joey and the rocks followed her. She began to detail every new design and feature of the house. Amy, Haley, and Ruth trailed alongside them. The walls were repaired, and there were painters working throughout the mansion, applying a fresh coat of paint on the interior walls. The roof was repaired, and the floors were replaced. There was still plenty of work to be done, but the mansion was in much better condition than when Joey first encountered it.

Joey turned to Mrs. Woods. "So, I assume you got the mansion back from Mr. Gregory?"

Mrs. Woods nodded, "Yes, we won the legal battle and were able to prove it was fraud."

"Ah, I see," Joey said, "I'm very pleased to hear that. Well, the rocks and I better be leaving. We will come back to visit you again in the future."

"Alright, Mr. Packard," Mrs. Woods agreed, "May good fortune allow us to see you again."

Joey and the rocks nodded their heads in agreement, and the butler showed them out the door. Joey bid farewell to the butler as they walked out. Upon leaving the mansion's park, they turned back to give it a final look.

"It sure is a lot better than when we first saw it," Roc stated.

"Yeah," Ks added, "It's weird how just a month ago this mansion looked like a complete dump."

"With the passage of time, things change, for better or worse," Joey mused. He turned away from the mansion, "Alright, Rocks, let's head home."

Outside the gates a taxi pulled up to the driveway and parked. A well-built man with square shoulders got out and thanked the driver. He pulled out several suitcases and walked up to the gates with confident steps. The man saw Joey and the rocks leaving the mansion and immediately stopped them.

"Ah, Mr. Packard," he said, giving him a firm handshake, "Is everything alright here?"

"Everything is fine, er…sir," Joey replied cautiously, as he did not know who this man was, "We were just checking on the progress of the mansion's restoration."

"Ah good, good," he sighed, "I saw you here and thought a robbery or something happened. Allow me to introduce myself. I am Ivan Woods."

Joey and the rocks looked at each other in surprise.

"I see renovation is well underway," Ivan looked at Joey, "I've many questions for you, Detective."

Joey chuckled, "Yes, Mr. Woods, I'm sure you do. Come inside and I'll tell you everything."

The two men walked back to the mansion chatting all the way. Ks looked at Roc and groaned.

"Well, confound it, so much for us all heading home."

"Mhmm," Roc sighed, "It's gonna take two hours for Joey to tell him the whole story. Come on, we might as well go home ourselves."

The two rocks sauntered down the path back to their apartment. The sun shone brightly upon them with white light. Birds sang in the trees and white puffy clouds floated happily overhead. On to the next adventure!

Narrator's Note

I see you have made it to the end of the adventure. Wonderful! Give yourself a pat on the back for your achievement. Our comrades sure had a hard time finding the real Ruby Cat. Gangs, thieves, and family affairs were a few of the things they didn't sign up for. The legend of the Ruby Cat is a real story that is often forgotten among the many legends of the world, swept up under a rug like dust and dirt, never to be discovered again. The reason it is considered a legend is that while there was a real jewel thief named Klaus Gudden, and the rubies themselves are a real treasure, the actual appearance of the cat he hid it in is a matter of debate. Michal Graves was certain that Klaus did in fact hide them in the statue, but no one can verify his claims. So, check your attics, basements, or even your grandparents' old house. There might just be an old cat statue in your possession, and who knows? Maybe the rubies from the Ottoman Empire might just be buried in the statue's clay, waiting to be discovered.

Credits to the Resources

Book by C.B. Colby:

"World's Best Lost Treasure Stories"

www.treasurenet.com

www.members.tripod.com

https://www.treasurebook.net/eyedcat.html

(The Spokesman-Review - May 12, 1959, Page 3)

https://news.google.com/newspapers?nid=0klj8wIChNAC&dat=19590512&printsec=frontpage&hl=en